What people are say

Secondhand D

Secondhand Daylight is written with the style and verve I've come to expect from Eugen Bacon and Andrew Hook.
Priya Sharma, award-winning author of *All the Fabulous Beasts*

Secondhand Daylight is a joy. It hurtles along at a cracking pace, is relentlessly inventive and always emotionally engaging. Both Green and Zada are spiky, flawed but eminently likable characters and the reader is quickly drawn to them and their individual plights.
Terry Grimwood, author of *Interference*

An innovative and gritty take on time travel, fate and entanglement. This story grabs the twin spirals of nostalgia and future-shock in one compelling bite.
Justina Robson, author of *Glorious Angels* and *The Switch*

In *Secondhand Daylight* Eugen Bacon and Andrew Hook resettle readers beyond the laws of physics. They unsettle its foundations, fundamentals and possibilities in a universe where time travel scenarios hold "no basis in scientific fact" and can "only be psychological". This is a bracingly versatile and provocative book.
Dominique Hecq, award-winning author, poet and translator

A cracking tale of puckering timelines that shimmers with possibilities and blesses with impossibilities.
Clare Rhoden, author of *The Chronicles of the Pale*

Beautifully disjointed and exquisitely nuanced, Bacon and Hook have deftly created a transgressive, dislocated narrative that will have readers losing hours with the efficiency of a time slip.
Dave Jeffery, author of the *A Quiet Apocalypse* series

Intriguing and poetic, this ambitious book combines hypnotic writing with a gritty cynicism reminiscent of William Gibson. Whether lost on the dance floor or to the mysteries of time, the story of the main characters' stubborn survivalism will pull you in and not let go.
KC Grifant, award-winning short story writer and author of *Melinda West: Monster Gunslinger*

Quantum Leap meets *Memento* in this clever exploration of time travel. The plot loops enticingly around an exploration of the personal impact of skipping erratically through time.
Phil Nicholls, reviewer and writer for the British Science Fiction Association (BSFA)

Hook and Bacon superbly capture what it is to feel out of sync with life. This is the new SF, a refreshing take on old tropes.
Tony Ballantyne, author of the *Recursion*, *Penrose* and *Dream World* series

Secondhand Daylight is a tale of characters entwined back and forth across time that picks Green and Zada apart as they try to find themselves, to discover purpose, and maybe find each other. Everything ripples off the page—words, phrases skilfully evoking place and character.
Scott Vandervalk, editor and author

Bacon and Hook's novel *Secondhand Daylight* is an emotive and kinetic take on time-travel fiction, where magical realism and hard sci-fi collide to form an innovative and poetic narrative which fans of 80s post punk and books like *This Is How You Lose the Time War* will certainly enjoy. *Secondhand Daylight* is subtly queer and tinged with social commentary too, showing Melbourne changing through the eyes of two distinct and well-realised protagonists, starting in the recent past, and offering a surprisingly hopeful vision of a future yet to come.

Maddison Stoff, neurodivergent non-binary essayist, independent musician and author of *For We Are Young and Free*, a collection of meta-fictional Australian cyberpunk

Previous Titles

Mage of Fools (Bacon)
Bacon's sentences are ceaselessly reaching with a boldness that would have made Angela Carter proud. Her stories are restless and relentless.
Angela Slatter, multi-award-winning author of *All the Murmuring Bones*

Danged Black Thing (Bacon)
Eugen Bacon is an exhilarating writer. Her work is daring, fierce, visceral and sensual, fast paced and packed with action, earthed yet given to flights of fancy. It is driven by empathy for the eccentric and marginalised, a simmering anger at injustice and inequality, and a deep concern for the big questions...A true original who glories in language and gives uncompromising rein to the imagination.
Arnold Zable, writer, novelist and human rights activist

Candescent Blooms (Hook)
Wondrous. Five stars.
Roger Lewis, *The Telegraph*

Frequencies of Existence (Hook)
Andrew Hook sees the world through a different lens. He takes often mundane things and coaxes the reader to find strangeness, beauty, and horror in their form; he colours the world in surreal shades and leads the reader down discomforting paths where nothing is quite as it should be.
Aurealis, Australia's longest-running speculative fiction magazine

Andrew Hook is an undisputed superstar of strange fiction.
Neil Williamson, award-winning author of *The Moon King*

Refreshingly original, uncompromisingly provocative, and daringly intelligent.
The Future Fire

Nitrospective (Hook)
Hook seems to approach the question of existence from a multitude of environments and personifications. The slant towards existentialist themes suggests a more contemporary re-telling of the ideals of Camus or Sartre
Xander Duffy, Dundee University Review of the Arts

Secondhand Daylight

A Novel

Secondhand Daylight

A Novel

Eugen Bacon

Andrew Hook

COSMIC EGG
BOOKS

Winchester, UK
Washington, USA

JOHN HUNT PUBLISHING

First published by Cosmic Egg Books, 2023
Cosmic Egg Books is an imprint of John Hunt Publishing Ltd., 3 East St., Alresford,
Hampshire SO24 9EE, UK
office@jhpbooks.net
www.johnhuntpublishing.com
www.cosmicegg-books.com

For distributor details and how to order please visit the 'Ordering' section on our website.

Text copyright: Eugen Bacon and Andrew Hook 2022

ISBN: 978 1 80341 354 9
978 1 80341 355 6 (ebook)
Library of Congress Control Number: 2022943492

A CIP catalogue record for this book is available from the British Library.

Design: Lapiz Digital Services

UK: Printed and bound by CPI Group (UK) Ltd, Croydon, CR0 4YY
US: Printed and bound by Thomson-Shore, 7300 West Joy Road, Dexter, MI 48130

We operate a distinctive and ethical publishing philosophy in
all areas of our business, from our global network of authors to
production and worldwide distribution.

Contents

Massive thanks to the following bands: Magazine, from whose 1979 album came inspiration and the book's title; Sonic Youth, whose 'Kool Thing' pinned me to a certain dance floor in 1991; and Low for the album *Things We Lost in the Fire*, to which I listened on a loop during the writing of this novel. And of course thanks to Eugen, for taking this idea and running with it.
—Andrew Hook

To Mama, Baba, *ahsante, nashukuru mno kwa kunikuza*—my deepest thanks for nurturing me. To Andrew, for your tolerance with my foibles in writing this novel.

To Scott Vandervalk, our first reader outside us—huge thanks for your crucial thoughts and stylesheet. To the team at John Hunt Publishing, for the scrutiny and care in helping us shape the manuscript to the novel it is today.

To our readers and critics—for thriving our dreams.
—Eugen M. Bacon

Somewhere here
Someplace other
on my mind

Green

Chapter 1

1990

I came to on the tarmac outside the Sarah Sands Hotel. I felt my feet, wriggled a toe inside my boot. I stood with caution, scratched my head.

The fog just happened?

I remembered the blinding light that threw me. I remembered a grunt that was mine. How I'd leapt high and backwards, then all the way in an arc bottom-first downwards. How I'd found and lost my possible girl.

I walked gingerly back inside. The suit with a line in his fade short crop looked at me as if *how?* You got in, got out past the bouncers. My eyes said *fuck off, that's how* rather clearly. The hulk shook his head. Right-o, I agreed. Best not to ask questions.

I showed my stamped hand. Could have stayed silent, but still. "Nothing to see here," I heard myself say, almost a growl.

The bunch of hookers sipping fruit-coloured cocktails at the bar was gone. Another DJ was whamming his thing.

So what's this, you're wondering now? It's a non-start, that's what.

My story has another beginning. There's no bluebell forest or an undergrowth, no rabid dogs on a leash or shit like that. There are beer bottles and empty crisp packets. And later, let's say maybe, there's an AI or a bot that's both a burden and liberty.

As if.

So here's how it starts.

Chapter 2

I found my feet in a crowd. Throngs pulsing to time-warp did it for me, you know? Lives in a distortion of expectation, rushing, rushing, always rushing. Stepping off a purring train, climbing up a moving escalator, hurrying towards...what?

I looked around. A crowd wasn't there in the train from Essendon on the Craigieburn line, past Moonee Ponds, all the way to Kensington, then Flinders Street Station.

I slipped my ticket into the slot. It popped up on the other side, as the barrier opened. I snatched the ticket, pocketed it. Exited the station through an arched entryway. Trams and horses moved outside the station's mustard-coloured Mumbai look with its lost ballroom cone.

The big clock struck 11 pm.

I was on an RDO. Rest days off were ace—if I knew one thing. Waged part-time too—at 27 years—that was fab. Not the money, there wasn't much of it. It's not like I needed much. No-one barking up my arse, that's what I liked about it. Meant zilch ambition, so what? I had no time for the world.

But the world had time for me. I'd just given up smoking, felt brand new. Lungs pushing in, out, easy as. Everyone was rushing. Not me.

I took the 71 tram to New Brunswick.

The Sarah Sands Hotel was unchanged. My haven of tranquillity. I knew it through and through: established in 1854—pub, bar, disco right there in the heart of Brunswick. Thursday nights, the indie disco. It was once my playground with Bateman. My smile was wry. Batey—mate for life, until marriage, kids and a solid job happened for him, ditched me to the solo party.

The hotel stood proud, vibrant inside. But outside it was unimpressive, really. It resembled a giant square cake with windows. It looked like a pretty thing someone had chunked without forethought onto the tarmac.

Still, the best scorched pepper on the menu. Roasted olives, rustic chips in vinegar, steak and ale pie with a finger-licky peppercorn sauce and buttered mush. A gobbler tomato caprese pizza too, basil, mozzarella and chilli.

I wasn't there to eat tonight, and the kitchen was by now closed.

Round the back by the doorway to the disco, two suits stood in cop cuts, trimmed hair all the way. The line was long, and the bouncers were looking to punish, wanting to start things with a rebel. Well, I wasn't one. Never a rebel. Maybe a little, those days of me and Batey; the world—what do they say?—our oyster.

I reached the suit whose fade short crop had a line. He checked my eyes, the set of my jaw for trouble. But you know me. I loosened myself, pulled a smile that was a little clumsy—a party trick. I honestly didn't like suits.

The block of a man stamped my hand.

Now I grinned. The joint showered a thousand reasons to smile. Crammed with girls clad in hip hop, baggy jeans and tank tops. Blokes high on platform boots and some goth look detained with studded belts. Some were gobbled in oversized shirts, like mine, or zipper turtlenecks I didn't care much for.

I strode past the pool table with its rowdy mob, walked all the way to the bar. A bunch of hookers I'd seen before, now sipping fruit-coloured cocktails, all lethal, in V-shaped glasses. I caught the eye of the tall barman with a goatee, the one they called Sinner—he wasn't mucking around, showed little emotion as he took and filled orders. His deadpan gaze said he didn't want you to pry.

"One single shot crisp vodka," I said, peeling from my usual taste for a VB. Slipped a twenty out of my wallet.

That's when I saw my possible girl.

She was a catch. Not a hooker, I didn't think. Her black hair, unlike mine, was dyed. I was one of those blokes who knew things like that about women. I knew from the dark gold in curly sprouts at the roots where it wasn't permed into a fringe across her face.

She was in a pleather jacket and wore sunnies. She toyed with a clutch bag.

I gave her my best grin. "You look like an Em. New?"

She smiled back, perhaps at my English accent. "Something like that."

I caught a whiff of her sweet watermelon breath from the martini she'd downed.

"Try the Sea Breeze," I said in boldness. "It's ace."

Not Em leaned over the counter, beckoned Sinner. "How about not a Sea Breeze?" she said to him.

"Say what you want."

Interesting. I wondered what she'd done to sour Sinner.

Not Em frowned, saw a girl walking from the counter with a fluorescent drink. And pointed. "I'll have one of that."

"It's a Woo Woo," I offered more trivia she wasn't buying.

"Sure thing. Now you're naming drinks?"

Sinner mixed, shook, poured, and pushed the flute to Not Em.

She turned, now faced me. "I'm gonna need you to pay for this."

"I feel the pressure," I teased, reaching for my wallet.

"How about I get it?" a man behind me said.

"Yeah, first dibs," said Not Em.

I smiled at fading possibility. "Close call," I said. "Stay in touch."

I downed my crisp vodka, turned away from the bar feeling a bit shit that another man was chatting up my possible girl.

Above, DJ Shazam was doing his shuffles. Oh, yeah. The chords of 'Kool Thing' were near. I took position on the dance floor. Threw my hands, shimmied in half a step, pumped my body to the wink of the lights.

"Come on!" I yelled at the beats.

A clock on the wall said it was 1.27 am.

I liked it when girls watched. I was clinical in my approach, pulled some best moves. Belly jingle, arms akimbo. Drop shot move to the flashing neon. I adjusted my body in jeans and the oversized flannel shirt. Anticipated the drums, the lights, each blink and flash of the strobes.

Someone did a glide, leap and jump, moonwalked past me.

"Scoring points?" a girl said.

I swirled. "You dropped in," I said to Not Em.

"Deep. You said to stay in touch. I didn't know how so this is the next best thing."

She'd ditched the pleather jacket and was squeezed in a tiny slip dress that was more of a camisole with spaghetti straps. She slipped near me in sneakers, not boots like most of the other girls on the dance floor.

Her legs were bare, no leggings.

She had good legs on her, I noted. Nearly said it too. The spaghetti strap dress was so thin, so tight, I wondered how it didn't burst.

She flowed to the music. "You're not trying," she said.

"Trust me, I'm an expert."

"Of what—guessing girls' names? We both know how that went."

She slow-danced on the spot in a grind and sway I'd never seen.

"Nice," I said. "You mean business."

"You like naming things—what's this move, then?"

"The Rage."

We laughed, two strangers sharing a moment.

DJ Shazam whizzed out a fast-paced renegade, some megamix, then—finally—the chords of 'Kool Thing' chimed. I did a butterfly move, and my possible girl did a quiver dance to the throb of my pulse.

It was just us, the rest of the dance floor out of it in that moment.

"Look." I leaned across the music.

Strobe lighting hit me as our bodies neared and it was voltage. I felt myself here, where, not there.

Chapter 3

I approached Sinner at the bar. "Mate. I thought DJ Shazam was on to 3 am."

"He was."

I blinked. Looked at the thinned-out dance floor. The clock on the wall said 3.07 am. Had I passed out all this time?

That's how it started, a season of outpouring.

Now I stalked Flinders Street Station. My black desert boots a soft shuffle on the concrete as I searched between the sheeted downpour to watch the trams as they came and went along designated routes.

Destination: New Brunswick.

A 17-minute journey that would take me back to the Sarah Sands Hotel with the dance floor upon which strobe lighting had blanked me out bum first on the tarmac for two hours, or fast-forwarded me into the strangest future.

I remembered how, bewildered, after giving the suit that fuck-off look, after Sinner's answer had befuddled me, I'd stood solo in time as the dance floor stayed empty and then repopulated to 'This Charming Man'—the opening of Mr Floppy's '100,000 Morrisseys'. The timbre of the song caught muso Smiths' fans mid-step, wrong-footed on the dance floor.

And just then I understood that something had *happened* when that strobe lighting hit me at the chords of 'Kool Thing', something for which I clutched no explanation or control.

That night, further down the room after the peculiarity, I was past the pool table when I again saw my possible girl. There she was, speaking with new friends. She didn't look my way, which was gutting, as I brooded about the fuck that happened. I'd drunk only one crisp vodka, smoked no spliffs. Maybe it was the vodka, never my thing.

Out of sync with the new song, I entered the toilet, rinsed cold water through my spiked hair. The force that threw me had coincided with the strobe, that much I knew. For a moment I was here, where, not there.

Now I looked about, another Thursday. I shook my head, craved the familiar. I leaned against the counter, caught Sinner's eye and ordered a VB.

Chapter 4

Two Thursdays now. Here I was again, bidding to replicate that night. Journeying from Essendon to Flinders to New Brunswick. I'd walked it once, a full hour and 18 minutes, a supermoon ascending over a bridge at a location I could no longer recall.

I danced to a megamix, butterfly-moved to strobe lighting.

But no. Nothing happened to leap me in the air and crash me bum-down on the tarmac.

It affected my output at the job in the factory, always distracted. And I'd had what appeared to be another time jump, didn't know why, but I was too startled to consider it.

It happened after a part-time shift. I'd knocked off work at 5.30 pm, waited for the 5.50 pm bus from Port Melbourne to Flinders Street Station. The bus arrived on time. I noted the young driver, a clean face fresh from school, because I noticed such things. A scatter of passengers, the mother with a toddler.

The bus hummed.

We approached traffic lights and the beam blinked amber, then red, and I felt a little dizzy by the time the lights changed for the bus to continue. In 19 minutes I'd arrived at Flinders, only the big clock said different. We'd arrived at 7.39 pm, not the 6.09 pm that would have been the right time.

A whole hour-and-a-half lost, and no-one seemed ruffled by it. Well, I was rattled, seeing that the driver (now ash-haired) and passengers (no mother with a toddler) were all different!

I wrapped arms around myself in the cold, and wondered if this was the life I'd convinced itself to be.

Chapter 5

Shrinks have a knack of asking, "Tell me about your mother." She wasn't true blue, which kinda made me fake. That's how I felt, sometimes.

Mum and Dad relocated in the mid-70s, leaving England just as music was about to break. I grew up feeling disconnected from a culture that was past, present and future. Who was I? What was I? There was a certain resentment there, one so solid yet stretching to my mid-twenties, I felt it an infraction.

With brown hair so dark that others thought I'd dyed it black, my wan complexion and tendency towards punk, my retained English accent and an unfamiliarity around camaraderie...oh, fuck it—I was an outsider. It was a badge I was proud of, yet it troubled me. I guess even the roundest of pegs sometimes sought a square hole.

The dissolution of my parents' marriage hadn't rectified the situation.

Mum returned to England. Dad dissolved himself whichever way.

Here I was, staying solo in the Essendon suburb, caretaker for a space of fermenting memories. Dad gallivanted to fruit-picking seasons in the Dandenongs to the north, shuffling on his knees at strawberry level or balancing at top-of-the-ladder height cutting grooves into his index finger as he snapped cherries from their stalks.

The house was a life some would envy: a vacant property to which I held no financial commitment. Remember? Zilch ambition. I used the space to expand a burgeoning record collection. On occasion, I brought some gal home.

I'd grudgingly come to respect my quick jaunts from the suburbs into Melbourne, and was cool with a part-time job at the Boeing factory that built wing parts. I earned a pittance that covered groceries and bills.

Yet, the walls of the house reverberated with the residue of arguments and recriminations, evening shadows conjuring Mum and Dad, fingers in each other's faces, or worse—thin walls no barrier for their subsequent making-up, the grunts and humps of a sex act that, even unseen, sounded as brutal as the arguments.

The paucity of Dad's means hardened into reality those transient memories. Much of the trappings of childhood that I did remember were gone, sold to cover bills and spousal maintenance.

I slept on a mattress on the floor in the corner of the second largest room, as if the proximity of two walls might offer emotional warmth. A mattress and three pillows on the floor, a stool here, a single chair there...The furniture was rudimentary at best. Whenever I tugged someone back here from the dance floor, someone like Not Em had the chance happened, it never bothered me that the one-storey property gave the impression I was squatting in my own house.

The cutie, whichever cutie, made good noise in that squatter house as I introduced her to the power of pre-orgasmic sex, as I licked her up a stairway to heaven, and put my tongue everywhere she allowed. Her pleas rose in urgency and crescendo while I held back and held back until she gripped my hardness and, with a moan, pushed me into her wet folds.

In a nutshell, my squatter house didn't seem to bother anyone else either.

Chapter 6

Thursday night I was back at the Sarah Sands Hotel. It afforded me an approximation of community. The post-punk crowd dressed as extras from a Cure video. The DJ who *knew* which records to spin, the dance floor which was my church. Within that rectangle, under multicoloured lights, cossetted by music, I spun and twisted, cavorted my body into memories and shapes, glimpsed others doing the same, amorphous companions who returned to the shadows once the song finished.

It was a dance floor that forged acknowledgements rather than friendships. I mostly kept to myself unless I was feeling especially voracious for squatter tantra to a roaring climax.

Yet here—in this specific space—I sensed a journey that might last forever, so inexorably did it stream. At the same time, I felt pinpointed in reality, a light moth pinned on canvas. Sometimes it was as if a gigantic *You Are Here* arrow positioned me on a map right there on the hotel and its dance floor.

The chords of 'Kool Thing' began and I took to the floor. I felt confused abandonment as the song came to an end without voltage, without me blanking out, or taking a single step in forward time.

Chapter 7

Three Thursdays later.

My journey to the Sarah Sands was now a distorted pilgrimage, not unlike those attempts to impose happy memories on the Essendon home. I slipped out of Flinders Street Station between raindrops to chase a nearly departing tram, its doors whistling. I shoved myself inside, stood gripping the overhead strap for balance. I trailed a groove towards what was now a windowed cake building where nothing inside it happened to toss me here, where, there, when the strobe lighting flashed.

I listened for 'Kool Thing', and jiggered nervously waiting for something, anything, to take me out of time, out of place. Tonight, the DJ spun 'California Über Alles' by the Dead Kennedys and, once again, I found myself lost in music, my body gyrating, backwards walking, turning, stepping, immersed in song. Everyone else faded to a blur, faces smeared red as if violently lipstick-kissed, those closer to me meshes of black clothing, some ripped and torn.

In the height of the song, I disconnected. Not in the time and space sense, but the waiting. The desire for something to happen undermined my expectation of movement. This wrong-footedness lost my grip on the music, sullied the experience, ruined it.

I spun off the dance floor feeling desultory. The world rearranged itself, someone else filling my space, as I became inured to the sounds, realised I was so eager for that time-shift to happen again that it destroyed the pleasures of the everyday.

I took myself to the bar. Got in a VB. Wasn't drinking vodka tonight. Fuck vodka. I sat alone and morosely near the pool table for the remainder of the evening. Songs I normally gyrated to were this night anathema to my ears.

I watched the pool balls clack and interact, their motion predestined with each hit from the cue but maintaining the illusion of free movement. The metaphor wasn't lost on me.

Long before the hotel closed, unusual for me, I was under the darkened sky. A possum rooting through a litter bin rustled the quiet of the night. I leant against the side of the building, molecules in the brick subtly shifting through the reverb of the music still playing inside. I took a couple of deep breaths and pondered why I felt so plummeted.

I knew why. That 'Kool Thing' moment I'd experienced was the equivalent of an illegal high. I understood now that what I craved was its kick, its repeat clarity yet haze, its affirmation. Nothing else would suffice.

The possum manoeuvred its way to the bottom of the rubbish and was now making a journey back. I held my focus on the bin, tethered reality. As the possum emerged, lights from a passing car caught its eyes, and the shimmer reflected me and my possibilities.

I blinked rapidly at the peculiar flash, felt a bit off. I stood away from the building then reached out a palm for the surety of the brick. The edifice crumbled under my fingers.

Chapter 8

I wondered at the back of my mind if I'd had a seizure. Some unknown epilepsy, accentuated by the lighting flashes, somehow hooked into the rhythm of the movement. The pounding of the dance floor reverberating through the soles of my feet, jiggling me forwards into a time and space that wasn't meant for dancing.

That possibility was likely, but I no more wanted to see a doctor than I did a psychiatrist. There was an embarrassment in being ill, a frailty I wasn't asking for. But if it were an ailment, it was a *good* thing. Because then it would account for the events of that night.

No-one had shown notable concern or curiosity, not the suits on the door nor the punters when I'd re-entered, but illness was the only logical explanation. And, with my English background and the clinical disintegration of my parents' marriage, I was less attuned to impossible fantasies.

Was that why I'd somehow let Not Em go rather than approach her where she sat with those girls, offer to buy her a watermelon martini or a Woo Woo? Was it why I now wasn't picking up girls, crouching them above me face forward on the floor mattress, sliding them into me, wrapping their legs around me in the most intimate way as I pulled into their G-spot?

I was losing my game. There was that yellow-haired Rapunzel in the unisex cloakrooms, the one whose name I couldn't remember. There was the chance with the older girl—Lily or Sweet Pea, whatever—who'd kissed me, both with her lips and her peony and sweet alyssum scent. I was holding off on hooking up. Nothing lasted forever and illness was a plausible bottom line that underscored facts. If I acknowledged epilepsy, then it would be a definition.

I deeply wanted to talk to someone, maybe Dad, or Bateman at the factory. Brainstorm and chuckle about what might be happening. But Dad was a ghost, a silhouette from my life, and I wasn't so cool with Batey any more. Nah. *He* wasn't cool with me any more. Bateman's life was now Tammy and the kids, fuck me. And Bateman in his supervisory cap was a broomstick up my stinkiest butt.

I thought of Aunty Dawn, Mum's sister. She'd once visited from England, way before Mum and Dad parted. Dawn was a fulsome little thing, tiny bodied yet vibrant with life. She wore the face of a comedian and had only to look at me a certain way to yank out my giggle. She came bundling bars of chocolate, and for a while during her stay I called her Aunty Chocolate.

Unlike my mother, Dawn wore no make-up—she floated around the house, in a space that wasn't hers but as if she belonged right in it, with her unmade face, everything about her just wholesome and free. But she understood the tension between my parents, and I overheard a conversation one night, as I pretended to be asleep, just before Dawn returned to England.

"Let me take him," said Dawn. "He'd love the English countryside. The boy needs wind on his cheeks."

Please, please...I'd silently prayed to all manner of gods, prayed quietly but earnestly under my blanket, so badly wanting an adventure to happen in my mediocre life.

But Mum wouldn't hear of it, was especially vocal about it. Dad appeared to consider it, but he too eventually said no. His refusal fell out like a stone, a weight that was killing him. It was as if, deep down, he knew I didn't fit into that life in Essendon. Their sex that night was animal, punishing, as my parents took it out on each other.

Pretty much after that, my mother upped and left. And my father first went mentally absent, then managed to translate it into a physical absence, fruit picking as far from home as he could go.

And I was all alone.

Chapter 9

Everything still, everything silent. My night was shadowed in moss, much too unclear no matter how sombrely I tried distilling notes and ripples, fists and elbows of the past, present, future. A car stopped out front, the engine dry and fading, and was now at the back of the house. The smell of hot sugar and a dread of borrowed adulthood seeped into my mindfulness. Would subtler distinctions emerge at some stage, I wondered, neither boys nor girls, adolescent nor old, just faces pondering at my window?

I watched cricket from my floor mattress and a cathode ray screen that my penny-pinching dad had pushed onto me when he abandoned living and wisped off fruit picking. I flicked channels and settled on an abridged replay of the day's Test cricket between England and Australia. Sunshine at the back of the Aussies offered me emotive release. Sometimes I felt conflicted about who to root for—I was, after all, a Pommy bastard. A part of me felt crushed when an English wicket fell. But I was also true blue, even if Mum had chosen not to be, and this team...wasn't it something?

The English were at the crease. The Aussies had this fast bowler, bowling shoulder and head, heights on a quick pitch, balls slapping onto the wicketkeeper's glove. That was just a warmer, and the batsmen panicked. There was nearly a runout and, in the end, England was bowled out for a mere 131 runs.

The Aussies took to the crease, the opening bat shuffling, swinging over the wicketkeeper to four runs, four runs, a boundary. The English brought in a spinner who created things, looked to hit the stumps or find an outside edge. He was a crackerjack, the ball fizzing and bouncing and turning, until it caught an inside edge of the bat and a fieldsman settled easy underneath to catch the ball.

I downed VBs. Considered for a moment calling Dad, but we hadn't spoken in a while, okay, years, and I'd no clue if my dad had the same phone number still. I didn't really want to know if he was fruit trotting at ten bucks an hour in Cairns, Tasmania, Freemantle or just across in the Yarra Valley.

A new roar in an appeal—another leg before wicket. The incoming Aussie bat was efficient at the crease, slashing at the ball to put it away for four runs, four runs, a boundary, despite aggression in the bowler who was sharp and giving it everything. The English field was under pressure, and cracked.

Just then, the screen flickered. Then it was as if I was watching a brand new game. The Poms were on top and whacking runs on the bat. Four, four, boundary. When their bowlers came in, the Aussie batsmen fell like gnats. Each fall of a wicket, the Aussie bats walked and walked off the crease, their heads hung.

Bloody hell. Sure, I was a bit hungover, well, a lot, but a hangover didn't change sport on screen. I looked miserably at the telly. The fuck was this?

I slunk beneath my blanket, slept ordinary, my breathing regular. Woke up to seven missed calls from Bateman.

Chapter 10

Now I sat on a train from Essendon, and it was painstakingly chugging and stopping at Moonee Ponds, Ascot Vale, Newmarket, Kensington, North Melbourne...all the way to Flinders. Where was the limited express when I needed it? The train was funereal, barely a passenger, even though it wasn't that early in the morning.

I wasn't anti-cars. It was simply a matter of economy: 1) I had no car park and 2) the annual licence renewal fee was bloody theft. Maybe I was a touch enviro. Emissions and all that, doing my bit to save the planet.

For the strangest reason, perhaps those missed calls, I measured how it was before with Bateman. We'd planned to go backpacking in Europe, chuckled at replayed recordings of the posh tube voice of a female operator saying: *Please mind the gap between the train and the platform. This is Chiswick Park* (chortled at how it sounded: Chiz-ick). *This is the District Line train to Upminster.*

I looked around the empty train now. No underground female voice telling me precisely where I was. Here, you had to peer at stations, crane to read the names on walled signs, and it was harder to read on a limited express train that whooshed past stations. One time I stepped onto a platform for a closer look, and the doors whistled just before I could jump back on. The train left me, and I was late for wherever it was I was going.

Batey and I had each scratched up enough for a plane ticket. I smiled wryly. Don't even ask, I thought to myself. I'd knocked off something, a fan or an aircon, I couldn't remember what exactly now. Maybe sold some of my records. Then I got some good hands-on bud, and weed always sold quick on the streets. With all that money, we went no further than Townsville and Noosa.

The horn of my train blew, and we pulled cautiously into Flinders Street Station. I stepped out of the gates, walked round the west block, missed and cursed a number 234 bus just pulling out to Port Melbourne, and had to wait 20 minutes for the next fucking bus.

Chapter 11

"The hell?"

I swirled.

"Enough already," gritted Bateman, now factory supervisor. He'd approached from a distance, and was so close that I could see tiny flecks of silver in his white-as-white teeth.

"Mate, I know I'm late—"

"Late? Where the bloody hell were you yesterday? Come to that, why are you here today?"

I blinked, caught in the process of donning overalls. "I don't get it, the big deal—"

"You don't come in, you don't call, you're worse than an ex."

I stayed standing, overalls half-mast, uncomprehending. "We're kind of exes."

"Don't fuck with me. I'm done covering up your ass. So what's the excuse this time?"

"I missed a bus."

"Mate, listen to yourself. You're contracted weekdays. Since when did you start working weekends?"

My tongue unloosened, my mind spooling. "Say what?"

"You gone stupid or something? Whatever you're on, flush it. I've seen blokes like you bury themselves. I don't want to be there crying tears, clutching a fistful of soil to hurl onto your coffin."

"What day is it?"

Bateman chewed on his answer. "Saturday, mate. What day do you bloody well think it is?"

"It isn't Friday?"

Bateman sighed. "You think I'm paid to repeat? Sounds like you lost a day somewhere. Now you're here, you might as well make up for yesterday. Unless you've got plans."

I shook my head. "I'm sorry, okay? I'm having lapses... missing time."

Bateman fingered the scar across his face from broken glass those many years ago in a pub brawl. A badge of what he got as a youth bar hopping and gallivanting with me. Lucky no-one had pressed charges then. Now he was burnt out, painting garden gnomes for a six- and a two-year-old. Rekindling on family barbies and mucking around, going *Arr me hearties* with a kid. Whipping rainbow sprinkles onto slobbery licked ice-cream cones. No wonder he was a fucking pain.

In whichever explanation of time, part of me was still meandering in Noosa and Townsville. Bateman had ambition. I didn't. That was that, no complexity. I was comfortable with the odd tantra here, there. Bateman found a wifey who came swinging out of her shoes, not closing an eyelid on Bateman, denying him leash. Soon as we set foot back in Melbourne, Bateman was tying himself down and popping out kids, getting a job at the factory, becoming a supervisor. Batey it was who got me the part-time gig.

Now he took a card from his wallet, handed it to me. "Here's help. Employee assistance and whatnot. Now, fuck off before I write you up."

I started heading off, then paused. "Uh..."

"What?"

I shifted my weight on a foot. "Tams and the girls, going good?"

"Breathing every day. Come around for a barbie some time."

"Really?"

"Bloody hell, Green. That was yonks ago we did that." Longing and a memory flitted for a moment on Bateman's face.

Then he slipped into his teasing smile of auld. "That will be all," he said. "Stay away from my daughters, you bloody pervert." There was no menace in his voice. "And leave me wife out of it, unless you're stating paternity."

I smiled wryly. How things changed. We came back to Melbourne, and suddenly it was summer, then autumn, then winter, then spring.

But life wasn't moving for me. Well, it was *moving*, just too fast and not where I wanted it to go right now.

Chapter 12

Batey and I, we'd driven north, pulled off the road and down a dirt track at random, so we could take a break and eat pre-bought meat pies and down a couple of tinnies. On a clifftop we'd glanced down into the sparkling azure and caught sight of a school of dolphins, their fins rising and falling in forward movement through the surf. No-one else around. A moment pure for us. At the time, I'd wished I had a girl there.

There was an aspect of growing up, growing older, but that was a continuation of societal expectation. It didn't have to be that way. Yet I was holding up this slavish adherence to the Sarah Sands Hotel on Thursdays, a devotion now cemented by the time-slip, a *need* to return to the scene of the crime to check if it would happen again.

But that was just as crazy as seeing my possible girl in a footy crowd, catching her eye as she sat over a hundred seats away, and then determining to return to the same spot week after week in the expectation of seeing her again. Yes, I'd done that, over almost the whole of one season, but of course that had never repeated.

Pinning hope on illogical situations, I was great at that. There was nothing stopping me from getting off the predestined train tracks and taking flight.

I'd once read a book that equated travelling and time travel. I remembered this line: *Lose track of time and it will lose track of you*. Maybe that's where I should be heading. Away from the city, the routines chosen and self-imposed…

"You daydreaming again, mate?"

Bateman's hard slap on my shoulder interrupted my thoughts. I almost dropped the machine part I'd been turning over in my hands, as if it were a puzzlebox waiting to be solved.

Since we'd ceased travelling together, I realised Bateman's outlook had become external while mine stayed internal.

"Something like that," I said. "I've been wondering if I should get out of the city, out of the routine. I'm getting stale, you know what I mean?"

"I don't." Then Bateman softened a tad. "S'up to you, mate. But hankering after the past doesn't mean that it'll make a difference to the future."

Bateman was right. Nostalgia for our trip and the freedom it represented was no different from hankering after Not Em at the club. I needed to create *new* openings, not those tethered to any kind of reality that I knew.

"I've been thinking about what I said earlier," Bateman was saying. "You up for a barbie next weekend? I'm not working the Saturday, and I'm sure Tammy and the kids would love to see you."

I nodded, less sure than Bateman was. I was a broken cog within that familial scenario. But it would represent a step into reality over and above my recent fantastical musings.

"It's a deal," I said. "Mid-afternoon?"

"Good man." Another slap on my shoulder. "Now get back to work you lazy Pom. These aircraft wings won't make themselves."

I was smiling, then I remembered I'd somehow lost a day, and frowned.

Chapter 13

End of shift I looked around for Bateman, but he'd already left. I caught the bus to Flinders, grabbed double-cream brie, some tasty cheese slices, thin-sliced salami and prosciutto from the Coles on Elizabeth Street for dinner and snacking at home. Guess I was a bit of a planner in a sense, and the fridge worked decent, so I grabbed a few things for Bateman's barbecue the coming week: a bulk pack of free-range chicken drumsticks, a loaf of cheap bread, beef sausages, chopped pumpkin, corn, roo burgers. I also bought some fresh milk for myself and a bottle of cheap red—a shiraz viognier on special, most likely passing its shelf life but Bateman wouldn't mind or notice.

Then I headed home on my usual train journey.

This time I got out at Moonee Ponds and walked the remaining 5 km. Every journey has to start with a first step, I told myself. Breaking routine any way I could was the start of transformation.

It was early evening, but the sky was still open and hot. I headed east along Puckle Street, glancing inside the fronts of stores that were beginning to close and restaurants that were yawning open. I considered grabbing a classic satay on rice at Jack's Satay Bar, but the grip of the reusable shopping bag was beginning to cut through my fingers, reminding me I'd already bought the evening's dinner.

Groups of kids hung out around the KFC, their faces goading me about how old I was starting to feel. I'd reached an age where I wanted more than silence. Those many years ago, as my parents fought, scratched and ripped at each other with words and hate, all I wanted was silence. Those years were long past but for me silence was still everything.

And the music I'd found at Sarah Sands Hotel was calming. Nothing kicking in my head, nothing piercing, shredding, tearing...just naked hum and metaphor inviting itself in the poetry of a nightingale. I found balance on the dance floor, became alive, truly alive, in the quietness of music. I found my feet in the heart murmurs of a platform-heeled, goth-clad disco crowd flowing to a DJ's moonglade.

But something was shaking that peace. Something foreign scratching and ripping at it, losing me time. I looked at the youths. The older I got, the more youngsters there were, I reckoned. I shook my head. It was almost the truth, just not quite. Seeing those youngsters, life ahead of them, I wished I hadn't passed up on internship jobs that had come my way, one in electronics. At the time, I'd reckoned there was a slim difference between internship and slavery, the no-pay, shit-pay thing. Not that I lived on air bubbles, eating nothing. Even nothing had a price, hence the part-time at a factory.

What was I at 27? Null ambition, that's what. But age was just a number, or was it? I laughed out loud at the falsity of the adage. Age had weight in it. See how young those kids looked in the late afternoon light. Give them 10, 30, 50 years, see what they became. Age wasn't just a fucking number. I could only hope for wisdom to come with numeri.

I glanced up at the Clocktower Centre. It was coming up to seven in the evening. Time hadn't jumped. My feet were aching by the time I reached home. I shouldered the front door where it had expanded against the frame, easing it open into the dark interior of the house.

I stood for a moment in the doorway, caught between inside and outside, between possibility and conformity, dust motes catching the sunset light in a mini-galaxy swirl. It became an effort to move forwards.

When I finally moved, it was with the sensation of pushing myself through solid air, as though every molecule in my body was sublimated then expunged through some invisible barrier.

I paused for breath, realised I was out of it. I kicked off my shoes and headed into the kitchen, placing the carrier bag on the counter. Even though I'd swapped the bag from hand to hand as I walked, there were grooves in my palm at the base of my fingers where the strap had dug in.

I lifted the contents, placed tinnies and jars in cupboards, the brie, salami, prosciutto and whatnot in the fridge. I opened the milk, took a gulp, and spat it into the sink.

The darn thing was spoiled.

Chapter 14

One week out.

I felt out of hands and rather foolish clasping a moth orchid bouquet for Tammy in one hand, the shiraz viognier for Bateman in the other. Naturally, I was whopper miffed that the shit Coles on Elizabeth Street had sold me decaying groceries. I'd had to chuck nearly the whole fucking lot, as in everything I'd got for the barbecue was pretty much stuffed.

I considered grabbing a pork belly on my way because Bateman did the meanest roast. Rubbed it with salt, soy, smoked paprika, cumin, brown sugar and a touch of garlic, then slow-cooked it for hours. It fell apart in your mouth and tasted sweeter than heaven. Yeah, no. I didn't want to risk an already tender situation by arriving with rancid meat. I'd managed to lay hands on a super pack of lollies containing Chupa Chups, Drum Dum Pops, Tootsie Pops and whatnot. The kids would love that.

I took the Lilydale line from Flinders, 50 minutes on the train to Ringwood. Strode my way to Nelson Street, where Bateman and his family lived in a townhouse with a wedding cake façade.

Look at that! It was as if Bateman had gone out of his way to emulate the Sarah Sands Hotel style. The house was a four bedder with three friggin' bathrooms (the heck did anyone need *three* bathrooms for?), two garages.

Short story, Bateman had done well for himself, left me scratching my arse way back on the no-progress lane.

I rang the bell, Tammy opened the door. "Oh, you," she said.

"Ahoy! Oh, Captain!" squealed a youngling, and I realised it was Ali. An eye patch and all curls. "Arr!" She slammed into my legs.

"Heya, how are ya?" I squatted to her level.

"Pretty," she said. "Where's the bounty?"

"This do?" I handed her the lollies.

"Arr! Cast in or cast off!" She clutched the goodies, but her mother yanked them away. "Ahoy, mine booty!" cried Ali.

"We don't do lollies before tea," said Tammy firmly. She opened the door wide for me, but her look said otherwise. "Please, come in." The invitation was cold. She flinched at my offer of the bouquet, sniffed at the flowers and scowled as if a skunk had sneaked one into the lavish arrangement.

She led me up a floor to a natural-lit lounge, all timber-floored. The sofas were all mahogany framed, plump cushioned in elegance. I took one look and just couldn't sit on them. The dining room was set with napkins shaped like flowers or something you could eat. The room opened to a stainless-steel kitchen with high chairs against stone benchtops. There was a coffee machine so sleek I could hear it making a latte, smell its roast aroma of crushed pods. But it was all in the head, 'cos the device said *don't touch*. It mirrored the house's moral imposition, its decisive unwelcome. I crossed the sliding glass door to a balcony, opened a folding chair and sat in the open air.

"Where's the big man at?" I asked.

"What's up with you?" Bateman appeared, as if on cue. In his arms he clutched the toddler, Zee.

"We said barbie, right?" His whole body language...I felt unsure. "I'd gotten some meats, but heck—"

"Just stop it." Bateman pulled up a folding chair, looked at me with such utter disappointment. "Mate, it's one thing to let me down. But Tammy..." he shrugged. "She cooked a storm for you."

"Mate, I'm here," I said. "You're talking as if I died."

"You show up a week later!"

"Wait, what?"

The toddler startled at Bateman's roar, at my outcry. Bateman rocked Zee. "Shhh, babe. It's all good."

"I don't get it," I said but, really, now I did.

"You're ridiculous, maybe insane. Last Saturday came and went. And the homeless had a feast. We've got lives to live, mate."

It took the air away from me. "Fuck!"

Bateman covered Zee's ears. "Language, we've got kids."

"I'm sorry, it's just—"

"Time lapsed?" said Bateman. His scorn was louder than the roar of "Arr, me hearties!" shaking the house somewhere inside, tiny feet going thump, thump, thump.

"Maybe I should dock it off your pay," said Bateman. He touched the scar on his face, but it was me that he considered with distaste. "You know what, just leave. Please go. I'm done with this nonsense."

"Mate. Come on! We've travelled a long way. I'll reach the bottom of this. Get me legs back. I don't know what's happening."

Bateman stood pointedly. He handed Tammy the toddler. Zee whimpered louder, reaching back for him. "Dadda..."

Strewth, it cut. The loneliness. It pieced me up then fell upon me like a crescendo of sound. The knowledge that I didn't have a family clinging to my neck like Bateman's did. I stood, feeling lost. And I didn't like feeling lost now, any more than I did as a child.

"Maybe I expected too much from you," Bateman was saying, marching with purpose down the steps to the front door. "Still got that card?"

I nodded. The hotline to a shrink.

"Used it yet?"

I shook my head, frankly out of words.

"Well, then." Bateman gave up on me.

Somehow, Ali was there, clutching at my legs. "All hand hoy! Aaarrrgggghhhhh!"

"Not now, sweetheart." Bateman peeled her off me, finger by finger.

"Aye, aye. Aaarrrgggghhhhh, me hearties!"

The door shut firmly to separate me from my once best mate and the little pirate.

I stood outside for a moment. I stood until the weather turned. It was unreal. A bolt of lightning flashed by my face, but at a time like this what did I care? It was like watching myself suffer, inside out, cowering all over again under a table, slipping beneath a couch as my parents killed and resuscitated each other. Only this time I was older, able to save myself, but no clue how. Something was dismantling me, pulling bits of me ahead in time, and I just wasn't ready.

I walked away from the house, felt eyes on my back.

I stood outside the station, watched my train chug past, then another, and another. I stood in the rain and let it pour on me, rumbles of thunder growling. I touched my face and didn't know whether it was rain, tears or rage.

Chapter 15

Six months.

All of them gone just like that, unclaimable, because for me only six days had passed. After the shit BBQ incident I returned home, kicking ideas over in my head, pondering how I might find a path out of the embroilment.

Sure, I was confused, soft-focused, out of sync with everyone else, but I was rational enough to know that if I *was* losing time then there was some explanation that couldn't be some science fictional thang. Shit. It had to be medical—something physical or mental, and I found I was veering towards the latter.

I spent the Sunday on the sofa, watching cricket, the news, anything *real* that wasn't a fiction, anything that adhered to a specific structure of time, watching the clock I'd set on top of the TV, glancing at it every few seconds, a notepad by my elbow where I made a mark every time 15 minutes passed, striking through each hour with a five-bar gate.

By the end of the day there were no anomalies, nothing to suggest anything other than I'd wasted a day loafing about. Was *wasting* time any better than *losing* time? At least one was wilful.

I was so wired by this point I had no answer to my own question.

Monday, I made two calls. One to the GP to sign me off work with depression. Two to the number on the card Bateman had given me.

"Sorry," the receptionist said. "Dr Zabriski is full for the next four months."

"Bloody hell," I cursed.

"We can put you on the waiting list?" the girl offered.

Why not?

I had to get my head together before returning to work. I didn't want to face Bateman again, and honestly didn't know how to communicate with him right now. If I was going to dissociate then I needed to do so fully. Take myself out of the routine, assess mental health. There would be triggers, sure, something that stumbled me forwards a minute, an hour, a week.

What *was* I doing when I was losing this time? I had concerns over psychosis. I'd once watched a documentary where a woman thought someone else was living in her house. She found used pizza boxes in her rubbish bin, moved objects, there were unexplainable debits in her bank account, things arrived she knew she hadn't ordered. The upshot was she had a split personality disorder. There were seven other persons in her head who congregated when she was asleep and together had been plotting to kill her.

I remembered watching open-mouthed, reality stretched to the point of disbelief, while medical professionals confirmed the diagnosis. Truth is stranger than fiction, people said.

Maybe *I* had a multi-person disorder, and one of my identities thrived in the future. I laughed, without conviction. That case study proved the strangeness of truth, and I had to face up that I was on a trajectory that emulated aspects of that diagnosis. Because the alternative, that I was actually travelling through time, held no basis in scientific fact.

Not only that but it was ridiculous, I thought. Who the fuck travels in time in such a stupid way? If I had that ability, I'd be investigating a future filled with sex robots and flying cars, or going backwards, checking out why the dinosaurs became extinct.

Hell, even finding out next week's Lotto numbers would be better than only skipping forward an hour or two. Although, for that to be of benefit, I'd have to return to the present, and so far this was a one-way journey.

Something that truly adhered to my mind that I had to be suffering from a mental disorder was that I never travelled *backwards*, never returned to my starting point.

No, the time travel scenario held no basis in scientific fact.

It could only be psychological.

Chapter 16

I took a tram to Dr Zabriski's rooms on Victoria Parade in East Melbourne. Zabriski's office walls were painted cream cheese yellow, the carpet a pale grey. Sitting at the reception, I turned the card over and over again in my hands. I looked gratefully at the receptionist. Zoe, her badge said.

I smiled at her, but she was busy punching, punching, furiously typing. Good Zoe, I thought. I'd got a cancelled appointment, something had opened up in Zabriski's diary. But I also wondered if Batey had something to do with the change of luck. Maybe called in first, giving them a heads up in his role as supervisor and insisting that my condition was chronic.

Across the waiting room, the receptionist-cum-secretary was punching data into a computer so fast, the keyboard keys tapped like a storm of locusts hitting a window. My mouth was dry, my heart tripping. My head felt outside of itself, one of those moments like in a car accident where you suddenly become an observer of your own life, everything happening in heightened slow motion.

Zabriski ran through some basic medical checks, completed both an early onset dementia and a cognitive function test.

"See me next Wednesday for results of the comprehensive tests," the doctor said.

I could tell from his face that he was satisfied with the initial results. He was the company-referred shrink, I knew, so there were two sides to this appointment: 1) that I was fit to continue work, and there was the less altruistic getting to the bottom of my condition 2) simply, that I was fucked.

My palms were sweating.

Now Zabriski put me on one of those reclining couches and sat facing me, palms on his lap, face telling nothing. He spoke, his voice modulated in an even, reassuring tone. "What do *you* think is happening?"

"Aren't you the shrink?" I couldn't help asking. I really didn't like being a lab rat, someone else's study, even though it might give answers.

"I know this is our first session, but on the face of it you're a healthy young man."

"Bloody oath."

"Has anything been troubling you lately, in the run-up to these...er...experiences?"

"Seriously?"

"You need to work with me here, Green. You came to see me for a reason."

"I'm losing time, but it can't be actual, right? It can only be my perception of time. So I must be blacking out, then not remembering once I wake. That's all it can be, right?"

Zabriski's face stayed blank. "That's an astute assessment. The fact you're able to formulate it is a good sign that you're level-headed."

"What?"

"We'll book you in for some further sessions, but first the results next week. Consider what might have sparked what you consider that first instance, on the...on the dance floor, yes? Any emotional trauma, anything connected to your past. You've said the relationship with your parents..."

I tuned out.

"Are you one of those shrinks who takes the 'tell me about your mother' route? Well, on that score, I'm fucked. She bloody left us, me and Dad. And he's fucked too. But that's for another navel gazer session, right?"

"You have a lot of anger," Zabriski said.

"Wouldn't you also? I'm trapped in a bomb cyclone, a winter storm that's a blizzard, and it's losing me time. I came here because I needed a shock absorber, doesn't mean I'm ready to jump on it blind."

I could map these future sessions as clearly as if they'd already happened. Zabriski was following a well-trodden psychological path, but I couldn't sit back and wait for the results. If there was trauma in my past, I needed to be proactive.

Right now, I wasn't. I was sitting in the shrink's black leather chair, my feet an inch from the carpet as though I were a small boy at a barber shop waiting to get my hair cut on a ten-dollar special.

Chapter 17

I left Zabriski's rooms feeling hot under the collar—if I was wearing a shirt, that is. I wasn't.

I wanted to follow the science through a forest of unprecedented time lapses, each lateral slip coming out for me as fresh news. But I just wasn't into shrinks, and this thing...

I tried to keep calm, to put morbid thoughts and carrion at bay. What I really felt was that I was living in double-time, split seconds, because who knew what would vanish itself next? Hours, days, lost like sycamore seeds. Memories deleted because their hours had skipped. How could I poke a day with a stick in the eye if it never happened, or I'd zoomed past it?

I went and sat with it at the tram stop, the frustration pent up inside, the regret that stole in, then out, and perhaps some hope for a remedy that filtered through. If there was a remedy, I felt nearly certain that Zabriski wasn't it.

I returned mid-afternoon to Essendon. I turned into my street, and a kid on a scooter winked a torch on me, which didn't help my mood much, skyrocketed my migraine. I wished it were Thursday already so I could lose myself to blinking red lights, electronic music blaring on the dance floor. But 1) I was trying to wean myself off the Sarah Sands and 2) a letter in my mailbox piqued my curiosity, and what was inside changed my perspective.

I had to sniff the envelope, flower scented and hued a dusty eucalyptus colour. It was a wedding invitation on semi-gloss paper patterned in moody rose gold. I looked at the text printed in high definition:

WILL & SHAREE
Joyfully invite you
To their wedding celebration

On Saturday 11 February 1991 at 3 o'clock
In the afternoon at
THE DARLING HOTEL
301 Rupert Street, Collingwood
Reception immediately after, at their home:
4 Turner Street, Collingwood

I studied the elegant photo of my father and a bohemian-looking woman with a wreath of flowers on her head. They were facing each other. The woman—what kind of name was Sharee?—was trapped mid-laugh on the lens, as she leaned into my dad, her touch affectionate on the lapels of his jacket. My dad's lips rested on her forehead in the most loving way, one I'd never seen targeted at me or at my mum. They looked happy and serene. They looked like they belonged right there, *together* on that frame and its frozen time.

I curled the invitation, crushed it in a fist and fumed, fumed, then opened it again, looked at the crumpled faces of happiness and serenity. The wedding was this coming Saturday, and a part of me frankly wanted to put some ghosts to rest. What was Dad—Will! No-one ever called him that!—doing faraway from Cairns, Tasmania, Freemantle or wherever the hell he'd been and now living in Collingwood?

Even if I were to attend the wedding, did I have time or incentive to go looking for a suit? I considered for a moment showing up, just to object when the celebrant said, "Does anyone object to this marriage?"

But on what grounds would I object—parental negligence?

And, right now, the idea of a tuxedo and a bowtie was too much.

Chapter 18

Saturday.

I delayed the inevitable until I couldn't sit back any more, a wuss, without altogether ditching the going. Already I was late for the ceremony—perhaps I'd purposefully stalled to make sure I wasn't there to object, because every fibre of my being was screaming to do so. What right did Dad have to his own happiness, when he'd left me for shit?

I was early—the wedding probably just about finishing. I marched straight to the reception and, unsurprising, when I arrived, it was awfully quiet at the Turner Street house. It was a big and grey period structure with flowered awnings.

Dad opened the door. The ranging fellow he always was.

"Oh," he said, as if I was the last thing he expected. The door widened.

Took my legs away, seeing Dad this close. He looked seasoned in a good-looking way. Kind of self-actualised, and it pissed me off.

Wordless, I wove past him and into the living area. I scowled at the plush Turkish carpet most likely christened with a romp. I peered at it with distaste.

"Well?" Dad said.

"Some hippie!"

"Her name is Sharee," my dad said firmly.

"Does Mum know?"

"She left us both. There's nothing to know."

"Renting?" I poked, prodded.

"Sharee..." Dad threw his hands in the air, as if that would tell me everything I needed to know.

To say that the silence that followed was a little uncomfortable was an understatement.

"How are you, son?" Dad's strong grey gaze.

He looked older, even though his hair was dyed. He had this mature look, the good kind of maturity that made you want to trust him.

"Where's everybody?" I asked, a little harshly, rejecting the familiarity, the offer to trust.

"What?"

"The wedding reception."

"Son. That was six months ago."

"*What?*"

The time gap was starting to stretch, I couldn't ignore it.

"A girl was looking for you at the wedding," Dad said in the awful silence.

"A *girl?*"

"Girl, woman…" He shrugged. "Maybe people have a reason to look when you don't show."

Sharee climbed down the stairs, the bump on her stomach leading the way. She was wearing a red maxi dress that swung. Its V-neck was rather low and met the swell of her motherhood breasts. I shook my head. The last thing I wanted to be thinking about my dad's new wife were her breasts.

Her smile was enveloping. It shimmered and pushed a smile out of me, swapped my rebellion with shyness. I felt a bit giddy.

"The prodigal father's prodigal son," she said in a voice of natural husk.

"About right," I said. "Do you sing?"

We laughed together. Who stayed long in rage in Sharee's shimmer?

"Tea?" she offered.

"Absolutely," I agreed, and allowed a cushie sofa to swallow me in its comfort. Even my dad loosened up. I found that I couldn't maintain frustrations in Sharee's presence, couldn't cogitate the time lapse into something that made any sense. I rolled with it, moved forwards with it mentally as well as physically, just as Dad had apparently done since Mum left.

Soon we were chortling and sharing my childhood stories over fresh mint tea and homemade honey cake that tasted even more divine than it looked.

"Remember that time we passed this building that had been abandoned for aeons, and it was night but there was a light under the door?" Dad said. "How you couldn't help your curiosity and pushed a hand under the big wooden door where the light was coming from, and you pulled back in a bolt, jumped at a dog's fierce bark inside? We could see its shadow under the door, and we ran so fast as the dog barked and barked?"

We laughed till we gasped. "I've never seen you run so fast, Dad. You left me behind!"

"Yeah, I was a shit dad."

It got all awkward again, and I started feeling wrecked.

I took my cue to leave. The parting with my dad was, anyhow, less uneasy than our tense greeting.

"What was that about losing six months?" Dad asked.

It was then that I nearly told him.

How the slippage was a fear and an excitement both at once. A bit like a first love and a pet hate, redundant, sometimes vital, now and then frozen in pixel. How over and over I reassessed my position and only fumbled with the sound that my world made when I turned off the telly.

It was the sound of loss, no comeback. A sound I couldn't let go. It stuck with me, plagued me on tantra-free nights when I couldn't sleep with words I might use in a diplomatic solution.

"Never mind, Dad," I said.

"Call me," Will said, his tone doubting his own words.

Was it that he didn't want me to call him, or was it that he understood I was never planning to call?

I didn't know if I could ever forgive this dad, the one about to be a new father, happily wed to bohemian Sharee who knew how to steal hearts, even mine.

On impulse, I shoved myself into my dad, thumped him on the back in a hug. I felt my dad cling and, for a moment, it was okay, and then it wasn't.

I released him. "This time you caught a good one," I heard myself say to Dad in a voice that wasn't mine.

"She caught me," Dad said.

On my way back home, I passed an op shop, open late, and something in its window display caught my eye. It was a pirate moneybox, sea green outside, marked with skulls and sharks, the white-bearded face of a pirate perfectly split with a padlock and key. Inside was lined with red velvet.

I got it for five bucks.

Chapter 19

Something brought me to Turner Street. I didn't know what it was. Yet I took a train, all this way, and now I'd arrived.

I hated that I still felt a connection with a father who'd abandoned me. Years now since my last visit—the reception that wasn't. That's right. Fuck's sake. How I was six months late. Since then, I'd wondered about Sharee, what baby she had. I'd hurt a bit for a while about that. About being replaced.

Wasn't that what dads did when they took on a new family—replaced you?

I turned the corner and saw the boy dribbling a ball in the yard. I stared at the kid, at first with resentment—this was supposed to be my childhood. Then with curiosity—what kid did my father, Will, raise this time round?

It kinda hurt. This wasn't my home. It would never be.

The boy saw me and grinned, gap-toothed. He waved.

Kid was okay, I thought. How did my dad pull that one out? I approached the kid with a smile. Pointed at his ball. "You're ready to go." Then at the boy's muscles. "Look at the build on you."

The boy stretched out his scrawny arms and looked at them. "Nah. I wanna get the body right," he said. Gazed back at me. "Like you."

"What do you want to get the body right for?"

"I wanna play at the oval."

I squatted to the boy's eye level—this squatting to kids was becoming a habit. We faced each other. "Those big hitters, they make 'em in the yard, boy. How do you reckon they got started?"

"I wanna play at the oval," the boy said stubbornly.

"You'll be a ripper."

"Yeah. I snap great kicks."

"What position do you wanna play?" I asked.

"Ruckman. Look!" The boy jumped up high, and extended his arms. "I can get to the ball first, on bounce."

"Who are you barracking for?"

"The Magpies."

"What?" I put a hand to my heart, mocking to stagger back. "Those shits—Collingwood?"

"I'm rapt about them."

"I know a mate who goes for the Lions. They'll bash ya," I said, speaking like the boy. I was surprised at myself. Connecting like this with a kid who'd replaced me.

"Nah." The boy thumped the ball with his boot.

"Woah, good one. You certainly boot it up. You've got the trip."

The boy fetched the ball and kicked it again. "I'm ready to go in there first. Try me, toss it." He ran to collect the ball, and chucked it at my face.

So I did what he expected me to do. I lay my frame back and fashioned a kick, hard. I watched with wry amusement as the boy lurched himself at the ball.

"See me come at the footy," the boy cried. "I'm ready to go in there first."

"You don't duck at the ball?"

"I'm not a wuss," the boy said. "I grab it, drive it home."

"Is that why you're bouncing balls alone, not banging drums in your room to 'Peking Duck'—seen it on the charts? That music rocks, kiddo."

"Yeah. It's all happenin' for them. Not me," the boy said.

"I bet they started in a garage," I said. "You know what else I bet?"

"What?"

"I bet you'll be a premiership player."

"Yeah. When I play, I get to forward quickly. Boot 'em goals. When I'm big, I'll be hittin' them smashers. Nice finish. Fans roarin' me on."

"My word. You'll be famous. What will you do with all that money?"

"Take a jet to the future."

I took a step back. *"What for?"*

"Win all them premierships, all the way backwards."

I laughed at the irony of it. Here was a boy who wanted my place, a leap into the future.

"I don't doubt it," I said. I rushed and got the boy in a sudden tackle. We rolled on the ground, the boy giggling. "First blood," I said.

I stood, brushed off grass. The boy copied me, a mini twin.

"I take a good kick," the boy said. "I'm good at space inside fifty."

"You've got to set it up," I suggested. Arranged the boy's stance. Stood boot on boot, rubbing ankles with the boy. "Then you finish on the left."

"Left foot around the body?"

"That's right."

"I can do it. Give the posts a good look, then it's a goal. A left footer, like this!" The ball shot into the distance. The boy chased after it. Raced back hugging it.

"What do you do when the other team is coming at ya?" I asked.

"Not panic?" suggested the kid.

"Atta-boy." I felt a strange pride.

"See, I'm ready." The boy threw his head back and roared.

"What are you doing? This is not the Royal Rumble, pay-per-view. It's footy, not wrestling."

"I'm getting the mojo," the boy said solemnly. He put his hands on my chest and shoved me back. I held my ground, but the child had all his body in the push.

"Not a bad result," I said, holding myself not to fall.

"Ya here for Will?" the boy said suddenly. "He's not here."

"You call your dad by his first name?"

"He ain't going by what else." Pause. "I know who you are."

"Oh, yeah?"

"I seen them pictures."

"Well then." I noticed a curtain in the living room move. Sharee? I wondered what she was thinking, seeing Will's boys having a chat. "I guess I seen ya too now," I said. "So I guess I'll be going. See ya around, Buster."

"My name's Shane. You can call me Shano."

"See ya around, Shano."

The boy gripped my arm. "You comin' to see me next week?"

"What's happening next week?"

"I'm tossin' the coin at a match. The Magpies." Shano's hand tightened on my elbow. "It's at the G."

"Yeah, nah," I said. Shook the boy off. "I'm not one for the Melbourne Cricket Ground."

"But you'll come?" Earnest eyes.

I ruffled the boy's ginger hair, carroty as Will's. Well, once — Will was all ginger younger. Now he was salt and pepper.

"You'll come?" Shano begged again.

"Maybe. I gotta head off, mate."

But Shane wasn't done. "You played ball with our dad, them days?"

"Nah, kid. You're the lucky one."

Eyes on my back as I left. I turned. "Say what, kid."

"What?"

"The bender. I reckon you got it. Good on ya."

But, see, I hadn't been quite honest. I'd been to the G. Once, maybe thrice. A whole season, actually. Liked how that player, Sidebottom, wheeled around and kicked the ball on target, straight through the middle of the sticks.

Shit, kid. I wasn't keen on making promises I couldn't keep. Leap into the future and crush the spirit of a kid left behind — waiting, waiting for me to show up.

Nah.

Chapter 20

Some say loss is gain. The day I lost my house was the day I lost loads more. I became a billionaire. Yep. Just like that. I didn't know it then, like heck. Had I known, I'd have sat still on the naked ground and considered with discomfort what I'd do with all that money. But how could I have seen it—cloaked as it was in an invisibility of time? I did sit still, pout in childish ways at how the world had blissfully overlooked me. I pouted, even as time knew and gave me wings that would fly me to a sky of burning notes.

How did it happen...the wealth? It's a long story I can tell short.

It started with a demolition notice. I tore the brown envelope, and read:

> In accordance with the Building Act 1984, your property fails to comply with the building regulations in the City of Moonee Valley...
>
> The council has the power of prosecution and enforcement in relation to noncompliant buildings, dangerous structures...
>
> ...apply for a review and a counter notice within six weeks of receiving this notice...

That's the kind of shit you don't want to be reading. And not in government speak, no. I looked at the date stamp on the notice: it was a year ago. You gotta be kidding me. I'd lost a whole fucking year.

I called the number, it was a friggin' pain:

Sorry, we can't take your call at the moment...

I called again—guess what it said?

We are currently experiencing bin collection delays. Thank you for your patience. The fucking line went dead.

I called again:

Thank you for calling...our team is currently attending to other calls. Please hold and we'll be with you shortly.

I held the line and might have gone to sleep with my ear to the phone. A click as I moved up an analogue queue. I perked up.

Thank you for holding. We will be with you shortly.

Another click. *We're currently handling a large volume of calls, but we will be with you as soon as we can.*

Were they for real?

Finally!

Welcome to the City of Mooney Valley. You're talking to Ash — how can I help you?

It took a few repetitions for Ash to understand my problem. Yeah, you're thinking *racist, man, engage with difference!* but there was a real language barrier. I was also blabbering rage and frustration, and it was coming out in Babel.

It took more time to establish my identity, Ash insisted, before she could discuss *personal* details. Once all was in the clear and I'd stopped going aggro, Ash pointed out that it was long past the six weeks to request a counter notice. She said something about a Section 8 notice, and a Section 77 notice, both of which, she pointed out, I'd failed to respond to.

You might understand that this was the point I barked for a supervisor, who got on the phone after a short wait. She spoke calm, but firm, the way you responded to ease a foolish child out of his tantrum. "The council now owns the property," she said. "It's in the listings for demolition."

I roared again, something about wait-till-you-hear-from-my-lawyer, I later remembered, even knowing too well that I didn't have a bloody lawyer.

The supervisor appeared to take a meditative moment, then said, "Mr—"

"Call me Green."

"Mr Green. In a show of good will, the council shall grant you compensation at the calculated market value..."

Okay...We were getting somewhere.

She directed me to the City of Moonee Valley website where I could fill out an online form with details of payment. I reluctantly hung up and wished I hadn't, nearly cried with more frustration than rage that I couldn't find the online form, until I clicked the last link a reasonably sane person would have thought to look:

<u>Planning applications and permits</u>

And that, in a nutshell, was how I lost my childhood home, and earned council compensation that went into my National Bank of Australasia account.

By the time the bank merged with the Commercial Banking Company of Sydney to become the National Commercial Banking Corporation of Australia Ltd, my interest on the term deposit was substantially increased.

By the time I lost time again to find that it was now the National Australia Bank, also called NAB, I was substantially well off.

Yep. On the way to billionairehood.

Chapter 21

I regarded myself in the hotel mirror. Since that first incident at the Sarah Sands Hotel, I'd transported nearly a decade and a half into the future. The money from the house compensation accumulated interest faster than I could travel. So long as the markets held, it was clear that years leaping forward in real time was making me a rich man. Imagine having a goodly sum invested across five years that for me passed in five minutes. I didn't need to see next week's Lotto numbers, didn't need to cheat. My wealth was swelling through purely natural methods. Let's call it Darwinian.

And I hadn't aged! I regarded my face. It was hard to keep track of exactly how much time had passed in what I decided to call my previous reality, where sometimes it was only a matter of days, weeks, months.

I'd only shaved a handful of times since this all began.

I was popping forwards, flashing in and out, only ageing during moments when I was *present*. It wasn't like getting on a bus and ageing incrementally by the end of the journey. One moment I was *here* and the next I was *there*. No physical trauma. At this rate I might advance tens, hundreds, thousands of years until such time as old age kicked in and I'd still look years younger, perhaps wearing a seasoned appearance like the self-actualised one my dad had worn next to Sharee. By the time I aged and died...

The consideration was dizzying. Everyone I ever loved and knew would be dead, and I'd still be alive! I was by now accustomed to the time journey, coupled with the fact that it was totally unexplainable and involuntary. I had no choice but to accept this new *reality*.

It was inevitable I'd be lonely. I could instigate relationships, but my forward motion would lose them. One moment I'd be lying with a woman, giving her a tantric jumping frog, missionary, yet raised. The next moment she'd be dust. Unless she was like me. Were there others like me? These thoughts rattled in my mind, but usually I had no time to properly consider them before I was *otherwhen* again.

The instances were increasing, that much was quantifiable, and it stirred distressing moments.

Chapter 22

It pained me to think of the pirate ship, how I'd turned up at Bateman's door...That was back in 1991. I was back from Dad and Sharee, knew I'd lost six months somewhere, found a sheaf of letters on the mat below my front door telling me the timeline had tripped some more. And that was before the house saga.

The letters were junk, unpaid bills, Zabriski's final report confirming no mental aberration, more letters from Zabriski — different timestamps, offering follow-up appointments, then those too had dried up. A couple of formal letters from the factory, querying my repeated, lengthy absences, a final one terminating my employment.

And then there was the handwritten note from Bateman:

Where the fuck are you at, man? Sure thing, last time we spoke wasn't sweet, but to clam up, bin everything? The hell are you, buddy? You don't answer my calls, or when I knock. Can you at least answer this note?

It was undated.

I'd dropped off somewhere between those six months that flew by the time I'd gotten to Dad's and the time it took to leave Dad's and Sharee's to get home. The fuck was triggering me? I had an inkling light was involved somehow (the strobe lights at the Sarah Sands, the traffic lights, the possum's eye, the kid's torch...), but, darn heck, no scientist was going to confirm it. Maybe nine months had passed?

I was grateful for the grace period the council had given me to vacate. Talk of bureaucracy! The urgent demolition notice wasn't so urgent, was it?

Inside, I looked at the pirate moneybox. It was getting late, the sun nudging the tops of the surrounding houses, colouring them that melancholy orange that reminded me of gulping down decent shots of Bundaberg rum, and the treacle I smeared across pancakes when I was a kid. So much treacle, when I lifted the pancake to wrap my teeth around it, stickiness oozed out the folded end and onto my school shirt, driving my mum nuts. She'd clip me round the head, hastily unbuttoning the shirt and throwing it into the washer, frantically sourcing me a replacement. She was about looks, what others would see.

Those childhood memories...tinted...now felt like another life.

I removed the pirate ship moneybox from the carrier, took myself down the familiar Lilydale line from Flinders, made my way to Nelson Street in Ringwood. The sun was hot on my back through the thin tee I'd picked from Brash's music store. It boldly flashed the cover of the Sonic Youth album *Goo*. The lead single from the album was 'Kool Thing', the song (together with a peculiar strike of strobe light) that started the time anomaly. The cover itself was iconic, with its pseudo Roy Lichtenstein black and white pop art-type image—one I'd learnt had originated from a paparazzi shot of Myra Hindley's sister Maureen and her partner on their way to court. Hindley was notorious for all the wrong reasons, but the T-shirt was distanced from that, and distanced me from reality with the song.

I approached the familiar townhouse. Damn! Batey had let the compound go. The front badly needed a paint job, and the grass in the yard was half a metre high. The heck? It was as unkempt as my house in Essendon. I didn't want to imagine Bateman was doing some time travelling too, and how on earth was Tammy putting up with the property in this state?

I found urgency towards the front door. The path leading up to it was crawling with weeds and brush. I kicked something, almost tripped. The wood was entangled into the woven grass. I grabbed it with both hands and pulled, thinking it a slat from a broken fence, then realised it was Ali's pirate sword.

My fists hammered. I tried the door but it was locked. I hammered again.

"Bateman!"

Was this how Batey called and banged, slipped notes at my place? I wasn't as organised as Bateman. No pen and paper in my pocket. I was about to turn and leave when the door opened a crack, a taut chain masking the darkened interior.

"Bateman?"

He peered at me. For a moment there was silence. Two friends, nothing to say to each other. Bateman looked haggard through the slim space of the opened door. I detected alcohol on his breath. What? Before noon? At least it was when I last looked at the time.

Bateman glanced down and saw the wooden sword in my hand. Something like puzzlement then anger flicked over his expression. I didn't know what to think. Abashed, I tucked the sword into the crook of my arm, pulled the moneybox out of the carrier.

"I came to bring Ali this." I didn't like how apologetic I sounded.

Bateman slammed the door so violently I thought he might crack it. Then the chain disengaged, and the door wrenched open.

Bateman reached for the moneybox, his fingers gripping it as you might crush a cola can. To my bafflement, he bashed the tin box over and over against the timber frame of the doorway, splinters flying like tiny arrows. The box dented, the sea green veneer peeled away, the pirate's face crumpled into an expression of hurt, and I could do nothing but watch.

Bateman hurled the box into the overgrown grass, nearly taking my head with it had I not ducked, and now turned his attention on me.

His eyes glowered. The punch hit me hard to the face, just missing my nose, nearly cracking a cheekbone. I reeled back, hand to a cheek that was already burning. I tasted blood in my mouth where I'd bit it, and more blood pooled around my tongue. I moved backward and tripped on a yellow, green and red garden gnome that stayed standing but glared at me with accusing eyes.

I placed a good distance between me and Bateman's fury. Was about to speak, but Batey growled first.

"What the actual fuck?"

His voice was slurred. There were tears in his eyes. This wasn't a Bateman I knew.

"Mate—"

"Is this a fucking joke? Some sick humour you've got there, Green. You disappear. You're not there for me when I've got no-one to talk to. Now you swan back here clutching that fucking box as if nothing's happened. Jeez, mate. No, not mate...just jeez. Why don't you fuck right off?"

I took in the dishevelment, the ageing, the lines under Bateman's eyes, the lack of sleep, the excess booze.

"Buddy. I don't know what's happened. Has Tammy left you? Has she taken Ali and Zee? I..."

"Taken Ali!" Bateman slumped to the doorframe. Slivers of the newly damaged wood stuck in his palm. "Fucking cancer took Ali, four months since, after all that treatment when we'd thought it had gone into remission."

"Bloody hell!"

"And where were you when that was happening, Green? Jollying yourself up in Queensland, at Byron Bay or sailing around the fucking Whitsunday Islands? Dropping responsibilities like flies, that's where."

"Jesus, Bateman, I didn't know..."

"Course you didn't. No news from you, while I'm trying to figure out how and why Ali's getting sicker, and Tammy is struggling to cope. Then the whole damn cancer thing comes around again. But you know what? It's nothing. Hear that? Nothing."

"I...I don't know what to say, Batey."

Bateman stared at me, wild. "Where the fuck have you been, Green? Time travelling shit? You can't expect me to believe you think only days, weeks, months have passed. Years you've been gone. What game do you reckon you're playing?"

"It's not a game..."

"Tammy warned me about you, not that it makes a shit of difference now. She left six months back. That's what love does to you—trauma of losing a kid. Not that you'd know that. You love something so much that you can't bear it when it changes."

"I'm so sorry..."

"Yeah. Be sorry! Ali's death fucked us up. Poor kid. She knew when she was going, we couldn't hide it from her. And believe me, that adds to the pain. So just fuck off, Green, seriously fuck off and never come back. Jeez, even Ali acted older than you at the end. Fucking stoic, she was. Not pathetic like you!"

Bateman re-entered his property, slammed the door bang!

I stood. Immobilised. Wished the sky could open wide jaws, close them and swallow me up. I had no control over this. Nothing was my fault. I didn't cause Ali's cancer. I couldn't have altered it. But I could have been there to support Batey. I'd abandoned Bateman who, right now, was giving me a good option to abandon him again.

But the friendship was too keen.

I pounded on the door. "Mate, don't do this. I'm not leaving you like this!" I hurled myself at the door with my shoulder, over and over. Then I sat with my back against it, my eyes and throat on fire.

The garden gnome glowered at me.

I felt a presence, and knew that Bateman was behind the door. Perhaps sunk on the floor like me, back to back. We sat like that, partners yet strangers, for I didn't know how long. It was a bonding and a parting that was forever.

Finally, I took to my feet, touched the door with my palm, pressed my forehead to it, then yanked myself away.

I felt shit.

There were no tracks, no way backs, just forwards in fragment. I was transitioning smooth as night, day, night into the future but it didn't feel that smooth. *I* didn't feel that smooth. Fuck it. I wanted to press DELETE all the way back to the exact contours of absence.

What was the point of it all? What was the point of anything?

An invisible time jump was urging me into a fully formed future from an already broken past in whichever philosophical sense you wanted to think of it, arriving me in nothing but shards.

Chapter 23

Now, in the hotel, in this tormenting future, I pushed that memory to the back of my head—its distaste as vivid as if it were all happening to me this very moment. I locked the memory behind the mirror that reflected my face. I contemplated my expression, my options, saw nothing.

Was I learning the lessons of my parents' marriage, how the best way to not let relationships hurt you was to avoid them? But Dad had unlearned the lesson and his karma—a full-blown picture of Sharee in it—was full of happiness.

Not me.

I was catapulting into the future. And I was whirling solo.

Chapter 24

Rose-breasted galahs perched on the branches of eucalyptus trees outside the hotel complex. I watched them from the dining area, pairs necking into each other, their heads bobbing back and forth, their loud calls punctuating the air.

I nodded as the waitress removed breakfast remnants. A big fry-up. Beautifully cooked farm fresh eggs, smokey bacon, grilled tomato and mushrooms.

It was exactly the normality I needed after the dinner I'd suffered. I'd frowned at the Kobe beef and lobster burger, with a side of creamy spinach in organic butter. An opulent sundae speckled with edible gold leaves — 24 carat! — when, frankly, all I wanted was a steak and ale pie or a scorched pepper steak with rustic chips in vinegar. Or just a tomato caprese pizza with basil, mozzarella and chilli. The fuck did I want a lullaby-softened Kobe beef for?

The Diplomat was a 3-star hotel complex with a man-made lake in a garish pink arising from real flamingos wading long-legged in it. When I arrived, a waiter had met me with a smoking welcome cocktail named Jupiter. It had a fruit base, tasted of bitters and smoke, and yes, it smoked. Maybe it was dry ice, but, Christ, it smoked. It came garnished with an orange and a maraschino cherry. I'd have murdered for a good old VB.

I'd been amazed at the 30 double storeys, 85 private villas, 250 luxury duplexes, one of which housed me. It boasted a spa and a personal masseuse and a dedicated powder room. The toilet was so clean I couldn't bear to sit on it until an urge after that bloody Kobe beef and gold-leafed sundae snatched away choice.

The 3-star came with beaded necklace chandeliers, and dragonfly lights everywhere. On booking, I picked and chose from a selection of 22 pillows, custom fit beds, Egyptian cotton linen, eiderdown doonas…all on a touchscreen.

The room toiletries were so pretty and sweet smelling, I wanted to eat them. I went for lemon myrtle and did my darn best not to lick the body lotion and the accompanying shampoo and conditioner in a take-home leather pouch embossed with my name. I wasn't sure about the remote-controlled music, curtains and lights, but wasn't complaining about the Rolls Royce shuttle service. Bloody hell: there was a concierge and butler service that offered shoeshine, and attendants looked at you with deeply wounded eyes when you were stupid enough to offer them a tip. And this was 3-star. What would I get in a 7-star hotel? A private tour picnic on Mars?

I had to put a special request to the chef for a "normal" breakfast. The chef who attended to collect the request in person was a shrew or a grizzly hybrid. Tiny but full of aggro, much insulted at my choice of "unsustaining food".

No matter, my belly was now full, straining against the belt of blue jeans. I needed a clothes shop, soonest, not to buy clothes of a better fit, but those of a modern style. 'Cos in this world, I looked Zinjanthropus.

You could tell how folk eyed my wear—like the doll-faced receptionist when I checked into the hotel complex. "That's some cool retro look," she said, handing me the tablet for a fingerprint that would give me access to all facilities.

I found that I'd flown in time over a pandemic, now a thing of the past, but it had left scars and amenities. Hidden fountains lurked everywhere, squirting you with an antibacterial spray as you entered a hotel, a shopping centre, a train, or a plane, and it squirted you as you left. Doors beeped if your temperature wasn't right. I tried to imagine but couldn't visualise those days of face masks and fear.

RAT kits for rapid antigen test—I read how once there was a shortage—were now excessive promotional items that sat untouched on a receptionist's desk, a doctor's waiting room, and in overflowing boxes with branded handouts outside train stations—promoting something entirely different from a virus, in vivid print on the RAT kit wrapper. Every workplace was mandated to have an on-site nurse who offered edible vaccinations in lolly flavours.

The gym incited my interest, to an extent, but no way was I signing up for the three-day Split Intensive—that was for gym junkies. I was content to amuse myself on squats, bend presses, dumbbells and a triceps cycle.

When I wasn't lamenting over lost time, the complimentary MacBook Pro laptop and printer on request that came with the room was pretty handy. I fired it up (well, just hovered a hand over the keyboard and it came alive), looked into theories of relativity, space-time geometries and cosmic strings.

Most times there was the usual gumbo of time travel as the movement between points in time, a speed of lifetimes and wormholes. I became a routine visitor on Q&A wikis, mostly those focusing on time:

Is time travel a crime?

What is the fallacy of time?

Know the five ways you can travel time?

Such was my frequency, soon administrators of some sites were inviting me to join their online team and contribute to updates and fact checks, of which I was getting increasingly savvy. I found promising sites with fascinating names like The Illusion, Transversable, Unphysical Reality, Baby Planet, or Time in Crescendo. They talked a lot about travelling back in time, not much about travelling into the future, and they all disappointed me. They were mostly run by kids with no real names, just handles like Cobaltdanger000, Utopiation217, Prometh669, SharplunarZ, DualTheoriz, DutyFlo877 and DryIceNahBelch.

What do you bet? I reckoned their real names were like Scotty, Callum, Beck, Richo, Maddie. Kids who only took time off a screen to do speed, backflips, switchbacks and frontside doubles with a scooter or a skateboard on rails and moguls.

One of the kids, SharplunarZ, said, "Dude, just SocialBox peeps."

I found social media sites where people connected or reacted to each other by "thriving", "swatting", "spacenoting", "pashing", "woohooing", and I figured "socialboxing" was another form of cyber reaction to someone. None of those emojis meant anything near their naming.

I'd stumbled onto a generation that created its own new language. I quickly learnt online lingo to fit into those message boards: WTF, IKR, SMH, TLDR, AFAIK. Had to chuckle at ELI5—if someone had to explain something to me like I was five years of age, then fuck off. IANAA was another funny one—who expected everyone to be an astronaut? But I found myself using it sometimes when some tosser lurched a curveball I didn't have an answer to.

I found a rabbit hole that started off well with a headline: "The natural human condition is moving forward in time, second by second. But do you experience unexplained blackouts?" I clicked on the dancing GIF and it sneaked me to a site on how to enlarge my penis. None of the girls I'd slept with had complained, so that was as good a cue as any to shut the laptop.

I resisted the Rolls Royce shuttle (damn!) and walked to the corner of Bourke and Spring streets, where I stepped into a fitted clothes shop. I suffered the keen seamstress's walkthrough of tieless shirts and creaseless pants.

"This..." pointing at a photo, 'is a long sleeve compression shirt...And this here is a muscle-fit short sleeve..." blah blah "...made of organic bamboo—we call it a mojo fit..."

"I'll have the slim button-up in a set of four, please," I said.

She stood me on an automated measuring platform that swivelled this way and that, hugged me here and there, tightened an arm around my arm, my wrist, my calf...Now I was facing out to the street, at a patisserie named Je Taime.

Just then I saw her. She was in a dusty pink suit, walking briskly to cross the street towards my side. She was older than when I'd first met her at the Sarah Sands Hotel. My body came alive when I remembered the good legs on her, naked without stockings, the spaghetti strap dress so thin and tight, yet it didn't burst as she flowed to the music, teased me with her words and slow grind.

"Wait." I moved to jump off the measuring platform.

"Please. No!" The seamstress grasped me back. "Only another minute and we're done, else we'll have to do the measurements all over again."

The minute was a lifetime.

When I reached the door, looked every which way, even ran a little in the direction I thought Not Em had briskly walked towards, she was gone.

I sprinted across to Je Taime, asked the woman at the counter. "The girl, dusty pink and four coffees—where did she go?"

"*Je ne sais pas, désolée,*" she said. "You want crumpet? Is good. Half price."

I walked back, glum, to the fitted clothes shop, where the seamstress mistook my interest.

"That was a future blazer suit. We can do one like that for you—it doesn't have to be dusty pink, but it can be?" She raised her brow. She took my silence for agreement. "Single breasted, fit yet loose. Removable sleeves with a button. You can clip off its legs into shorts, inside out to a raincoat..."

"The fitting—how much?"

I cut through her monologue, harsher than I meant to be, my disappointment this much.

Chapter 25

Some girls stuck in my mind, some didn't. Some I looked at, passed. Some were pivotal. I'd been a late bloomer. My *otherness*, my English accent, my reluctance to have friends over in a house filled with arguments and recriminations, meant that happenstances during school years never transfigured into semi-innocent fumblings every other boy or girl seemed to accentuate and brag about.

My first kiss was one that came to me, not one that I took. A peck on the cheek in the unisex cloakrooms from a girl with yellow hair whose name I could no longer remember. Innocent, effective, somewhere between my jaw and my cheek, then she ran off before I could even consider reciprocating.

Afterwards, I'd entered a cubicle, sat on a toilet fully clothed, and touched my face in wonderment.

Then there was the older girl — made up to the nines, bouffant 80s hairdo, fishnets, pink rah-rah skirt, blushing boob tube under a white jacket, wreathed in perfume — who was always at the bus stop opposite the school waiting for her boyfriend at lunch times. I'd tail after other boys in my class, and they'd pop over and try to chat her up. She seemed so much older than them, but was probably late teens to their early teens. She was affectionate, funny, mostly enjoyed the attention those pre-pubescent kids lavished on her. From her perspective, it could have been endearing.

Then one day I found myself jostled from the back of the group to the centre, hands pushing my back towards her amid hoots of "he wants a kiss, kiss him". A look I couldn't decipher entered her eyes, as she studied me. Slowly, deliberately, as if in slow-mo, she leaned close enough to smell me. Close enough for a waft of her peony, honeysuckle or sweet alyssum scent to mess with my atria. She positioned those red lips and touched somewhere between my jaw and my cheek in almost the exact place where the blonde whose name I couldn't remember — Lily, Wisteria or Sweet Pea — had kissed me in the cloakrooms. Equally innocent, equally effective.

I pulled away, fled, wiping the lipstick with the corner of my dark blue sweater that clung onto it stickily for the rest of the day. What should have been elation was burrowed in deep-rooted shame that perhaps it was a pity kiss. Her unchanged gaze after the kiss, how she drew back with lips still perked, the formations of a smile curling, and the other boys' raucous laughter and lugubrious whoops...all summed up to make it worse.

Was her name Sally-Ann? Sharon? Suze?

If she were my first love, albeit accidentally, then Nicole was a premeditation. New Year's Eve, 1987. Drinking in PJ O'Brien's Irish Pub on Southgate Avenue. A group debating music and film. Nicole was there with an older friend, but I gravitated towards her, determined to kiss her before the night was out. Short brown hair, goldstone eyes, skinny as a rake. But did I even have a type? Yet something in the smile...

By midnight we were mouths touching, fingers at the back of our necks, then my hand palmed to her hip. Some fool shouted, "Green's scored some sugar!" and I felt like punching them in the face. What I felt was so much more than a sugary score.

We swapped numbers at the end of the night, pity Nicole had an exclusive sold-out party to attend. She never got in touch, neither did I. We never connected again, but I could picture her today — right now — as she was then, unaged, unaltered, smiling and making me feel a million dollars.

Perhaps Not Em moved my core, curling in over and over, closer to the chambers of my heart, because — like the chance girls — once again, she was a might-have-been rather than an actually-was.

I sat in the hotel room, newly bought clothes on the bed beside me, reminiscing precisely about how she said, "I'm gonna need you to pay for this." The texture of her hair, dark gold in curly sprouts at the black-dyed roots. The look on her face, giving back much yet little.

She was the last possible girl before everything spun out of control.

The kid on The Illusion said something about SocialBox.

I abandoned my room, found the receptionist at the hotel complex check-in desk.

"So this SocialBox thing…" I said.

"MacPlay, download the app," she said, not explaining beyond that.

Back in my room I fired up the Mac, looked at the screen. Right there on the desktop was MacPlay, a shopfront with a range of apps in alphabetical order. Too easy, there was SocialBox. The app's inbuilt help and tutorial taught me to get live feeds, to make and post my own live vids. All I had to do was look at a blinker and talk to the screen.

I perused other live vids. There was one of a young couple in a remote jungle, filming a search for Bigfoot:

"Save your lives, your future. Sasquatch is coming," the woman whispered, big-eyed on the screen. "Habitat is everything, and people are killing the forest. What will Sasquatch eat next? You." There were only three views on the screen, suggesting me, the woman and someone else were the only people to witness the live vid.

The climate video from a scientist in Oymyakon was fascinating but it too had less than 10 viewers. There were three "swats", one "pash" and a "woohoo". "Global warming has transformed our world that once saw the coldest temperature of −67.7 degrees centigrade, and now you'll be lucky to get −38 in Antarctica's South Pole…"

I felt stupid, unclued about what I was doing. The apps prompted for a series title. I mentally ran through a few names: The Grass Is Greener on the Other Side, Greener Pastures,

Green Future. Then gave up punning on my name and settled on Jumping Time. I sat back. Ran sound tests for clarity.

"Hi, my name is Green...This is Green of Essendon...Testing, Testing."

I deleted each, not liking the sound of my voice or the expression on my face, which was pretty much the deer in the headlights one.

Then looking at the blinker on the screen, I spoke clearly, feeling a little freer than I'd ever done.

"My name is Green. I come from the past. In October 1990 that's when it started, one night on the dance floor at the Sarah Sands Hotel in New Brunswick, Melbourne, Australia. There was extreme light, and then blackness, and I travelled forwards in time by a few minutes. Since then, I have been jumping time. The instances are incrementally greater, as I journey days, weeks, months, years into the future."

I stared at the blinker.

"In early November, I visited my mate Bateman at Nelson Street in Ringwood and discovered that I had lost a whole week. My father's wedding to his new wife was at 3 o'clock on Saturday 11 February 1991 at The Darling Hotel on 301 Rupert Street in Collingwood. I skipped the ceremony and went straight to the reception at their home on Turner Street and I found that I'd missed my dad's wedding by six months."

I blinked, feeling real sad.

"I've missed a lot of things in my life, and I'm sorry that I was not there for Bateman's daughter, Ali. I missed the whole COVID-19 crisis—that's a good thing, right? I'm not kidding and I'm not crazy."

I stared in earnest at the screen. "I didn't ask for this flip, this lope into a different time. It just happened to me. If you know what's happening, and why, please contact me. If it's happening to you too, let me know. I need to leave a trail, a sense of connection."

Pause.

"I don't know when I'm going next, but I'll be here on Jumping Time, talking to you when I can. I'll describe my surroundings, how things have changed. For you, it might be years before you hear my voice again, for me it will feel like minutes."

Pause.

"Keep tuned. Keep listening. If you've just joined us, this is Green, I come from the past. Until next time."

Had I said enough? Too much? How long before national security officers came thumping at the door, hauling me off to some research facility to poke and prod at my DNA? What would they cut, plug me to? Worse—what if no-one, not a single soul, saw my message? Condemning it to yet another obscure cyber feed like the Sasquatch and Oymyakon vids, blended and gobbled up with all that "thriving" and "spacenoting", misplaced with thousands and billions of human stories on SocialBox.

I lay back on the bed, closed my eyes, waited for something to happen.

Chapter 26

The past sometimes calls, shadowed in tongues and fingers ridden with moss, admonishments, regulations. Why couldn't I let slumbering dogs be? Whatever it was, some inner answer or wayward wind pushing into a frangible forest gusted me towards a stooped stranger inside an aged care home.

Moonee Ponds Retirement Home was a large Victorian building shelved on the outskirts of town. The outside was a front for an entirely modern interior that bore a virtual reality ambience in immersive hues and optimised sounds in what appeared to be visual, audio and tactile stimulation apparatus. Everything that might once have been decorative was stripped out to become modern and functional, techno wheelchair access and floating transporters for the aged.

An outdoor rehabilitation spa with devices appeared to be for working muscle knots and resuscitating hips, in lieu of replacement therapies. The retirement home was antiseptic in design, clinical in its futurisms.

I gazed at the pool for a while, understood it was a definite attraction that wooed more clientele, and I could have sworn a whisper of music accompanied the pulsing lights shimmering from the multi-sensory pool.

I strode up to reception with a confidence I didn't have inside. Why *was I here*? I questioned myself over and over. And why *today*?

I remembered the adage: as one door closes another opens. But my impression was that I was opening doors ahead of me so fast that I wasn't closing anything behind. And if there was one thing I needed more than anything, it was closure.

The middle-aged woman behind the desk wore a sheen on her skin. She looked blissful, relaxed, as if working in the wellness facility was therapeutic in itself. I imagined she was likely just a baby when I was a teen. I still couldn't get around the mechanics of ageing vis-à-vis my time jumping. I noticed her name *Janet* on the innocuous badge pinned to her lapel.

She looked up, her beatific smile. "Can I help you?" she asked and looked at me personally, an angel right there, giving me her full state of mind. She was reassuring, even as she suggested an inaccurate yet inclusive option for me.

"I take it that we have an appointment?"

I mulled for a moment on the word "we".

"I'm here to see Dr Zabriski."

It was easy to track the doctor down. He'd retired from the medical profession and technically wasn't a doctor any more, but still called himself one. Rightly or wrongly, a title was a badge of honour, the reward of an accomplishment, an identification. Something that I lacked, and always would. Identification. I had no real identity. If I did, with everything happening, no identity felt like my own. Who was I? *What* was I?

But beatific Janet didn't seem to question much. She looked down at some notes. "Ah, you're the nephew, right? He'll welcome a visitor. There's no-one else in the family, as you know."

I nodded. I'd struck it lucky with this visit.

"Peter, is that right?" said Janet. "Peter Zabriski?"

I grunted something non-committal, unwilling to carry this opportunistic white lie too much.

"If you'll just sign in here, I'll walk you through to the day room where the doctor is resting at the moment."

I paused. "Does he know I'm coming?"

"We've told him, but whether he'll remember..." Her voice tailed off, just as Dr Zabriski's life had done. "His dementia..."

This made my visit a complete waste, then, if the doctor didn't remember jack. Janet's black patent shoes clicked across the tiled flooring as she led me through the facility that was visibly an extrapolation of medical science, psychology and therapeutic treatment. Patients' faces slowly tracked me as we walked, as if I were the ghost in this place, and not the memories of their former selves.

The building itself certainly wasn't depressing. It was light and airy, decorated in soft pastel colours. Floating walls and natural light windows let in sunshine. Just walking, I had an illusion of a heavenly cloud, serenely wrapped in invisible sound.

We turned one corner and into a scuffle. A female in their nineties had struck out at another resident and was now gripping her wrist so hard that they were both yelling.

"One moment." Janet moved fast to give the orderlies a hand. Together, they gradually parted the two women and a nurse gently guided the perpetrator to their room, while Janet spoke softly and kindly to the victim.

She joined me after a while. "Another safeguarding to write up," she smiled. "They don't seem to realise all the paperwork they cause us."

"What was that about?"

"What's anything ever about? They're usually the best of friends. Neither of them will remember this in the next five minutes. A head massage is also calming. What I wouldn't give to be absolved of my own sins so quickly."

"Sins?"

But she gave that elusive smile again, guided me firmly but gently into the day room, and I understood she wasn't inclined to explain herself.

Dr Zabriski, my one-time shrink, sat in a sort of golden egg sofa, ensconced in its gold plates as it gently massaged him head to toe. He was dressed in a loose robe that almost resembled a kimono, and wore a face of tranquillity. At his hands was a control pad, and he could tap on the keypad, or use his voice, to switch flick across channels on a monitor before him.

Janet placed a hand on Zabriski's shoulder.

"Doctor? Your nephew, Peter, is here."

Zabriski looked at me so long, I began to worry. His eyes were rheumy, the green irises like lilypads floating in oily water. If there was recognition, it didn't show.

"I'll leave you to it," said Janet. Her shoes click-clacked back to reception.

Zabriski's mouth moved as though he were chewing on something. I said nothing, uneager to pre-empt conversation. I wondered what Zabriski knew.

"You're not Peter," the shrink finally said.

"No. I'm not."

"You've come for your second appointment."

"You remember me?"

"Of course, I remember you." There was a crackle at the back of his throat, a deteriorated voice decoder, his once even, reassuring tones absent.

"Do you remember what I came to see you about, Doctor?"

Zabriski tried to speak, and words hovered. His lips opened and closed like those of a dying fish, but eventually the words came.

"You're that one, delusions of time travel," he said. "Nothing was wrong with you. You were pulling a furphy, any excuse to get time off work. Why not just ask for a sicky?"

I tamped down anger. Intelligence and arrogance often went hand in hand. And I couldn't blame Zabriski, who'd been conditioned to see firm solutions to specific problems. My problem wasn't specific. Fair enough—who could deny that my circumstances were rather...peculiar?

"Do you think I've changed?" I kept my voice calm.

"Thrown off the delusion, you mean?"

"No. Have I physically changed?"

Zabriski looked me up and down. "Good haircut."

"Are we in your office? Look at your hands."

76

Zabriski's eyes followed the floating contours and virtual reality feel of the day room. He looked around, at the other residents in their golden egg sofas and soft tremors of full body massages, the technology panels at their palms, and sleek monitors in front of them.

He regarded his hands, their veins prominent between softened parchment skin. "Still pulling a furphy, young man..."

"You've aged, I haven't. How do you explain that, Doctor?" He blinked at me. "Time has passed," I said, in earnest. "More time than is realistically possible. You didn't see me last week, or two weeks ago. You saw me four decades ago, Dr Zabriski."

But the doctor only blinked at me, no recollection even of the current conversation. It was as if he had lost his train of thought and his fingers absently tapped on the keypad.

Then Zabriski seemed to gather himself. He shuffled in the seat, sat a little straighter. He looked directly into my eyes, and said, "I see you've come for your second appointment."

We sat companionably for another 30 minutes. Zabriski's thoughts wandered in and out but didn't touch on me or my past again. He spoke of his daughter who'd just started high school. Gemima. I imagined she was married with children by now. But then Janet had said Zabriski had no family. I wondered about that. Did Gemima exist? Was she dead?

There was fluidity of time here, in this room of residents surfing their memories, real or imagined. I could almost laugh. I fitted right in. Everyone was a time traveller here. For once, I was not the exception.

When I shook Zabriski's hand shortly before leaving, the skin was as soft as a newborn's. I strode softly back to reception, shaking my head slowly as I walked.

Janet was still at the desk. "How did it go?"

"As far as things go," I said, "it went."

Chapter 27

I longed for the familiarity of my record collection back in Essendon. I reminisced about my merry Aunt Dawn—my mum's sister—who'd visited us at the house in Essendon those many years ago on a trip over from England. I remembered her first words when she saw me in Australia, that visit.

"My, haven't you grown!" she exclaimed, as if growing was an abnormality, an unlikelihood.

But her acceptance of me was complete, and I remembered fondly how I called her Aunty Chocolate. I remembered with heartbreak how she wanted to take me back to England with her. She should have.

My, haven't you grown. I found myself holding to that phrase in my mind for some time, feeling guilty about it, as though I'd somehow betrayed my aunt by ageing, as though I should somehow have remained a little boy.

I imagined she was dead, now. For her tiny frame, she'd been much older than my mother. Later I realised that, for her, it was the distance in time that had made my growth look so sudden since she'd last seen me. The years had heightened everything.

This was my life now. Bateman, Zabriski, Dad...they'd all jumped in age even if it wasn't that long in real time since I'd last seen them. That disconnect was always there. The anomaly.

Chapter 28

Was it curiosity about the anomaly that lugged me back to my old school?

I stood outside Essendon Primary on Raleigh Street. It didn't look old, for sure. The entire building had transmuted. It was no longer brick built with the front tapering to a wooden architrave triangulating the roof, three arched windows looking out like a tuatara with its parietal eye.

The left-hand side of the school was now extended. It too was no longer the brick pillars that supported a wall of glass on a lower floor. The whole school had morphed into a structure of metal slats as a purely decorative piece of modern design and looked like a space station. I assumed there were classrooms up there too, but couldn't get close enough to be sure. And however nonchalantly I played it, hanging outside my old school wasn't a cool thing to do.

The kids were in high-collar blazers and slim pants in outfits that came out of the costume room of a science fiction movie set. They no longer wore the red tops and black trousers that Batey and I had donned. I remembered burning a hole in my sweater once, going back home and draping it across the top of my bedside lamp to create some *ambience*, only realising my mistake when an acrid smell began to permeate the room. I'd stuffed it at the back of the airing cupboard, but of course my mum found it and swore at me. Quick thinking, I'd blamed a chemistry experiment, a spillage. I couldn't remember whether Mum took the matter up with the school. After that initial flare, her usual flare, she probably wasn't bothered. What was a mum who was never a safe place?

Batey was my only sanctuary in those days. Despite my *otherness*, the Brit accent and dysfunctional family, Bateman, with his dominant outgoing personality, had somehow welcomed me.

Now I watched as the kids entered the school, arriving singly or in pairs, some driving the kind of cars I'd never have imagined possible. I watched them form reattachments once they were through the gates, linking up with mates, like I'd done with Batey, yet they were not doing schoolkid stuff like kicking a ball or jumping rope that kids did in my past.

These ones carried themselves with the surety of scientists on a mission, singularly focused to enter the learning. Despite all this, there was a universal feel to the school that made me realise how life moves in cycles of repetition. A cycle of repetition I was cutting a swathe through, a shark passing through a shoal of fish.

I thought wretchedly back to my friendship with Bateman, a friendship now obsolete. How we bundled across the school playground together, sharing Yowies and Dunkeroos, gobbling dark chocolate cake decorated with icing and sprinkles from Bateman's tucker box, the kind of lunch a kid got from a mum who cared.

I wondered about Shano—what the kid was up to. Did he break into footy in surging play? Launching at the ball, driving it home.

Commentators roaring:

"Never in doubt!"

"Clean off the boot!"

"Jams it through."

"Just pure!"

"What a finish!"

A tear stung my eye. Laughter from the school ground underscored my frustration. What the heck was the point of time travelling if you couldn't share it with anyone? What was the need for memories when they were yours, and yours alone?

Chapter 29

There were still no hover cars but sex robots were in development. I had wealth to fund prototypes. But mine were fragmented experiences. Thoughts and feelings lost in the corner of an ice rink. And this was not a play on words.

I felt cold. Literally missed companionship. Being with a woman, feeling the back of her knees, her thighs. Seeing how she responded to touch. How, when I found her G-spot, moments before her eruption, I swallowed her quiet or words that fell out of her lips. How she called upon her gods, her mother, whimpered, squealed or grunted an obscenity. Sometimes she whispered a basic y-e-s. YES.

I strolled the city, looking for...what?

The façade of Flinders Street Station hadn't changed. Still the same prominent dome, arched entrance, tower and clocks. Travellers waited for each other under the clocks, a literal time-honoured fashion, even as they held glowing devices that could tell them more than the clocks could. A café latte in hand, I watched them, all those people standing or flowing about, and I wondered how old some of them were in real time. Technically, they were a generation younger.

The time travel was a head fuck, that's for sure.

Between sips of coffee I checked out SocialBox. It was old hat to me now. The technology and my use of it intuitive.

People with time on their hands were responding in real time, some saying, "Jeez, mate." Others, "You're a Neanderthal." Others posting horror stories that were most truly made up like the one who claimed he woke up to find himself hatching in a crocodile's egg. No-one turned their screen on, preferring anonymity, clinging to those ridiculous usernames like Barridade57 and RetroCharm996. Some wanted to chat, not about time travel, but to sweet-talk or ask for money.

As had become key, I asked during the recording, "Hey mate, what's the date?"

"Seventeenth July."

"And the year?"

"The year? You got Old Timer's disease or something? It's 2028. All the way 'til the 31st December."

Yeah, kids took the mickey out of me, 'cos that's who I was talking to, I was sure. Kids.

Life had thrown a shoe at me. I hoped these interjections would reinforce my experience, make a true connection with someone potentially time jumping too. If nothing else, maybe I just wanted the world to notice me. I yearned to leave a mark, a footprint of existence.

A while back I'd sought to imprint the Sarah Sands Hotel. In the late 90s they renamed it Bridie O'Reilly's, then it was a bespoke hotel in the early 2000s. On that last visit it was back to its original name and purpose: a proper local pub in the heart of Brunswick.

But it wasn't how it was. The new Sarah Sands was clean, upmarket. The cake on the gravel look was gone. Now it was glints and sheens, soft arcs everywhere.

I put an order at the bar, and it wasn't with Sinner but a slip of a girl who wasn't born when I used to frequent there. I'd ordered a beetroot salad, with endive, radicchio, roasted and raw grapes, candy walnuts and Meredith goat's cheese. My tastes had changed too.

Now I finished another live vid. The day was my own. As they all were. I dug hands in my pockets, unsure of what to do. I looked at my financial and investment portfolio. It was healthy. I looked at the share market. SocialBox was doing well, unlike a new kid on the block: AI Evolution. It was a new starter, clearly limping. No backers appeared to trust it. Was it altruism on my part, or a sense of recklessness? Perhaps it was a feeling of doom, that whatever I did, what future did I have?

I put 80 percent of my investments into AI Evolution, the rest I transferred to SocialBox.

A chime told me of an incoming private message there:

"Maybe I can help. Let's meet."

I'd seen enough hoaxes to want to distrust Us3r-Z.

"How can you help?" I asked.

"I might know how to stabilise your jumps."

"How?"

"Reset in a four-dimensional wormhole."

"How?"

"Three pm tomorrow. Je Taime, 1–5 Bourke Street."

I waited for them to say more, but there were no other communications.

I closed SocialBox. After a moment, I opened it again, made another live vid: "I might have contact. I'll be at Je Taime on Bourke Street, 3 pm tomorrow. Bloody oath, can't wait."

Chapter 30

I woke from a long sleep. The house stirred, came alive with me. Not creaks and groans. Lights blinking, the giant wall TV sighing, petals softly opening in the silhouette of a pale blue flower animated into a screensaver. It shapeshifted into layered data tunnels in the shimmer graphs and pixels of a digital interface.

I looked about at a whole new room that did not resemble my abode in the hotel complex at the Diplomat. This bedroom was an empty white room, hexagonal, my bed a cubic backdrop against whose mattress my frame perfectly snuggled.

"Good morning, Green," my voice said in automation.

I looked about.

"I'm here," my voice said.

"Where?" I asked.

"I am there."

"Where?"

"I am everywhere."

"Who the heck are you?"

"I am you," my voice said. "Always you. Please step into the hygiene station, Green."

Fuck. I was subsumed in AI, a futuristic house that talked to me in my own voice. I didn't know how I felt about the spray of wind that dry-washed me in the "hygiene station" that A I Green walked me to. It was like a cool blow-dryer that was both refreshing and soothing.

"Let's put something over the birthday suit, shall we?" said A I Green.

A walk-in cupboard appeared from nowhere, and I stared at the assemblage of asymmetric tunics and cloaks, body fitters and baggies, most in black retro or off-white colours.

"In case you're wondering, you have a penchant for the slim leg, black boot look," said A I Green.

All pants were slim-legged with smocking, and they came matched with black, shiny boots that were equally cyberpunk.

"Will we be going out today?" asked A I Green.

"Out?"

Curtains dissolved and I gazed out at a megacity in metallic green shimmer. A glider resembling a kite or a bat, but it was a vessel, passed noiselessly by the window.

"Are those—?"

"Sonic-gliders, yes. Made of hollow material criss-crossed in struts and xtreme lightweight," said A I Green.

I touched my forehead. It was a bit overwhelming. What I truly felt like was a note that had lost its music. A letter on the wrong doormat. A house without a street. A mother who kept forgetting her child. There was no chronology to my jumps, just forward. I took each blink with a sense of panic, fearing the worst. Sometimes the ordinary met me. Unimportant, until it was. Sometimes the extraordinary, like now, sprang at me. Flaps in blue and white doors seeping uncorrelated lyrics that fell with intuition and abdication. I found myself having to adjust. Rearrange bars in twirls and admonishments, sharps and quarter notes, rests and dynamics...always closing on the accidental or a shuffle just before a cue or a breve. In this inner, outer country of what self, all I wanted was the familiarity of a treble clef. I yearned for clear mnemonics to *every good boy does fine*, on sheet (not shit) music that was never random.

Here was another future.

"What year is this?" I asked.

"Twenty-fifty," said A I Green. "To be precise, today is Thursday 19 May 2050. Will that be all?"

"Are you a butler or something?" I asked A I Green, somewhat in annoyance.

"Something is a pronoun. A thing unspecified or unknown. I am not something," said A I Green cheerfully. "I am you."

The neon data mural still danced on the screen.

The house moved with me. The far walls of my bedroom shone like backlit mirrors and simply pushed further backwards as I walked towards them. Then they dissolved into more bedrooms, three kitchens, more hygiene stations, four dining rooms, and many offices.

There were mirrors everywhere, and I couldn't escape the salt and pepper in my once black hair. Marionette lines, like those I saw on my dad last time we met, how they matured Dad's face, not unpleasantly, I supposed.

A platter of pills and cubes appeared on a dining table, courtesy of A I Green. "Breakfast is served."

I looked at the capsules in bright and cheery hues: greens and whites, greys and mauves, reds and lilacs all calm on a black plate. I popped a red and white one gingerly onto my tongue. And it burst into flavour. Smoke and fat lit my mouth. It tasted of bacon. A brown and white capsule came rich with the earthy taste of mushrooms. A pink and red one bore the sweet and tartness of a fruit, perhaps mango. I looked at the clear coffee — it smelled and tasted like an espresso — but resembled water.

I wanted to scream. Where the bloody hell was normal tucker?

The future was *regression*!

Suddenly I noticed the embossed logo on each wall: SocialBox.

"What's this?" I asked A I Green.

"Why, it's your company. SocialBox," said A I Green. "You own many things, Green."

I looked at the ancient scythe graphic that was part of the logo.

"It's a Saturn symbol, Green. Of karma and justice. Your emblem is a horn owl."

"A horn owl," I echoed stupidly. "Does anyone work for me?"

"They are waiting for you right now," said A I Green.

A wall dissolved and I found myself in a board room. Two young people seated at the round table stood as I entered.

"Green," the young man in a cyberpunk tunic shook my hand. "I am John Roc, Chief Information Officer." He gestured. "And this is Tula Bludge, Senior Scientist."

Tula wore a sheer maxi dress, hooded, and—save for her inner black clothing covering some bits—I could see everything.

"Did I hire you?" I asked, unsure of myself.

"Zada did," John said.

"Zada?"

Tula pointed at a wall portrait of a woman staring ahead in a side profile shot. She was unmistakable.

"What's her role at SocialBox?" I asked.

"The Safiri Project, sir," said Tula. "Zada and I have been working on it. She's been attempting to unravel you."

"Unravel me?"

"To follow you back through your timeline. In your last SocialBox vid you mentioned meeting someone at Je Taime. Who was it?"

"Us3r-Z," I said incredulously. "But it never happened. I must have...time jumped." I scratched my head. "How do you mean *follow me back*—Zada?"

"She's tracking you. We did wonder if you'd...time jumped after that vid. Especially since there were no more posts on Jumping Time."

I felt my reality slipping. "I must talk to her. Now."

They looked at each other.

"You can't," said John. "Zada's travelled to the past."

"The past?" I almost shouted. "She's *physically* following me *back* through time?"

"To stabilise your jumps," said Tula. "And figure out how you travel forward."

"How the bloody hell will she find me?"

"Jumping Time, sir," said Tula. "You were very...thorough on your timelines. Zada is trying to loop back into your times and locations."

"And what bloody good is that? Well now I'm here. Tell her to come back."

Again, they looked at each other.

"We...can't," said John.

"There's no way to communicate with the past," said Tula.

"Then set the...time machine, what which *thingo*...surely, you've got something. She can't be jumping on beans. Whatever you use, *bring her back*!"

"That we can't do either," said Tula. She looked at her hands. "You see, the Tesseract is only a prototype. There's just one of them and it only goes backwards to pre-set times. Never forwards."

"The *Tesseract*?"

"It's a four-dimensional wormhole in a cube inside a clutch purse—"

"*What?*"

"We've been experimenting on warp drive and dimensions of space for years. Planes of possibilities. We found how to vibrate in dimension. A bright flash and you're in the past in less than a second."

"People are travelling to the past?"

"Not people, just Zada," said John excitedly.

"That's absolutely brilliant," I said, feeling far from elation.

"That's what we've been trying to tell you, Green. We did it! The Tesseract cube of dimensional travel. Zada figured out the dimension quotient. Travel in 7th dimension."

"A prototype, you said. Are there side effects?"

They looked at each other.

"Will you," I almost barked, then more quietly, "just stop… looking at each other like…that?" I almost said "idiots". "And give me some straight answers. *Are there* side effects?"

John cleared his throat. Tula beat him to it.

"Temporal memory loss," she said. And added quickly, "It eases in minutes."

"And how the fuck are you funding all this?" I asked, waving at the board room, at everything.

"You, sir," said John sheepishly. "Your investments. You own the project. Even in your absence, we figured you wouldn't mind for the experiments to continue."

"And why would you figure that?"

"Otherwise you'd time jump, over and over, to a nothing future, sir."

I slumped in the chair. It was green plastic. Or something resembling plastic—was this not an evolved world, climate conscious?

The seat moulded to fit my contours.

Chapter 31

The beginnings of a headache were coming on. It was understandable. I doubted anyone ever had to assimilate so much before. It wasn't just my time-slips that needed to slow down, but the processing of information, too.

I needed to catch up, like pronto.

"Let's back up a little bit. And don't call me *sir*. No-one's ever called me sir in my entire life."

"Of course, si…" John bit back on the last word.

"This *nothing future* you just mentioned. You can't see *into* the future, right?"

Tula shook her head. "No-one can. We can't travel forwards. Only you seem to have that ability. That's why you funded the Safiri Project—in the hope that someone would figure out your time-slips."

"But you haven't figured it out?"

"Not going forwards, no. We don't know how you're doing it." Tula frowned at me. "Do you?"

"I wish." I knew nothing other than an involuntary disconnection amid a passage of light on a dance floor, on a bus, on the street and scowling at a scooter…

"What you're telling me," I explained it to myself slowly, though it sounded like it was a question to the two youthful faces before me, "is that, unless Zada meets me in the past and figures out how I'm travelling forwards, then she'll be unable to return to the present? To *this* present. To *now*?"

"That's right," said John.

"She's fucked," said Tula, as if she couldn't help herself. "I told her!"

I ran a hand through my hair. "But that's a suicide mission. Who the hell but a nutcase or an idiot would volunteer for that?" I looked from John to Tula. "Would *you* do it?"

They looked away from me.

Then John said, "But others would. Others with less to lose or those with a greater sense of adventure. Those who want humanity to push forwards, to do what they can for all of humankind. Just look at the manned mission to Mars…"

"Mars? Has that actually happened?"

Tula broke in. "About three years ago. A one-way trip. Those astronauts know there's no hope of returning. So why do they do it? To carve out a piece of history, to push humankind forwards, to see what no-one else has seen…"

"Or to run from something. So Zada is either foolish, virtuous or running."

"You could say that."

"And me. I'm just a loser who can't help himself. I have no control. Which brings me back to the *nothing* future. How would you know that there's nothing?"

John shifted uncomfortably in his seat. "Well, we don't. But from your podcast it's clear that your time-slips are speeding up, whereas you're physically ageing in real time. You're what, just short of thirty-five now? You've experienced a handful years of real time but are now — is it sixty? — years ahead from where you should be."

I had nothing to say about that. Fuck it, nothing. I'd had nothing to say about any of all that fate falling on me from the sky, time jumps hurling at me.

"So what happens when you go forwards again?" asked John. "Into 2070, or 2170 or 21,170? What are you going to find out there? Will the world still exist?"

I shook my head, not in answer, just in acknowledgement that I was pretty much fucked. In real time.

"If we can stop it or even slow it down," continued John, "then at least you can live the rest of your days in something resembling the humanity you were born into. I don't know if you've thought this through, but can you imagine being in a future where *nothing* is recognisable?"

I sighed. The problem was, I couldn't bring myself to imagine it. Predict how humanity might develop or alternatively crash and burn, a probability that nonplussed even experts. That was the trouble with the future.

It hadn't happened yet for anyone to fathom it.

"But if Zada meets me…the past Green, will I be here, and there? Will I cease to exist here? If she can somehow puzzle out what's happening—together with this Tesseract thing—then, maybe, it'll work out?"

For a moment, I felt true elation. Hope. This shit might stop.

They didn't meet my gaze.

I ran a hand through my hair. "How long has she been gone?"

"A little over two years."

"Why didn't she wait for me here?"

John raised his hands in a timeworn gesture of a shrug. "We could only track where you've been. We didn't know if or when you might get here. There was no way of knowing if you might connect with our present."

I thought this through. And wondered about that brief connection with Zada that had befallen me in what now seemed like those many years ago.

Chapter 32

I sat on the edge of the bed. A I Green had already asked me—again—if I was going out today.

"Switch yourself off," I politely said.

"An off is inaction, out of which is not action," said A I Green. "But I can hibernate or pop myself offline for a timed period."

"Could you do that for a couple of hours? I'd prefer to be alone."

"You're never alone with yourself, Green. That's why you wanted me in the first place."

"Just power down, will you? I'd rather not be talking to myself right now."

"You're the boss. See you at lunch."

There was no noise to indicate A I Green had "gone". I was at a loss. Was I truly alone? "Are you still here?"

"I'm voice activated, Green. If you want me to stay offline it would make sense that you didn't continue speaking with me."

"I see I've given you my acerbic manner. I'll keep schtum. Come back online at twelve."

There was silence again. The temptation to break it was intense.

I wondered if A I Green was also programmed to record my movements, to monitor time-slips. Was his purpose anything other than to be a virtual assistant? And whose side was he on? I remembered an encounter with Siri a couple of time-slips back that had really wrong-footed me. Passive aggressive Siri had dialled me the wrong girl. A moment of weakness when I'd wanted an escort. Siri didn't think so. The delivery of a lemon pavlova was not what I had in mind when I asked Siri to dial Lemon. And that wasn't the worst of mishaps either. When I'd first interacted with Siri I hadn't even realised she wasn't a real person.

Talk about catfishing!

I stood and walked over to the wall that doubled for a window. There were those sonic-gliders again. What else was out there?

Zada. Not Em. She wasn't out there.

But I had no desire to go exploring. The novelty had rubbed off. I thought over what John said. What the future might *really* hold. For the first time since this forward time started, I wasn't simply confused, disorientated, or even excited. I was really fucking scared.

And this woman, Zada, had travelled into the past just to find me?

There had been an intimate frisson, right back at the Sarah Sands, one she presumably wouldn't have had at the start of her journey from the future. How did the past connect with the future? Was what we'd shared on the dance floor the chicken or the egg?

The loss I felt deep in the pit of my stomach told me I'd never find an answer to that question. Were there other interludes when Zada and I might have connected? Was her desire to volunteer born out of scientific curiosity or some inexplicable quixotic inclination? So many damn questions.

If our roles were reversed, would *I* have travelled into the past? Come to that, would I have volunteered for a mission to Mars on a one-way ticket? I knew the answer to that one, and in doing so, knew the answer to the rest.

I was nothing special. Just an ordinary guy with some aberrant ability that—in the grand scheme of things—was utterly useless.

I fell to the bed. I felt lethargic, lacklustre. I wondered if my dad or Batey were still alive. How old was Sharee's kid? Where was my mum? Did she think about me and Dad every now and again? I craved that she did. There'd been nothing from her once she'd returned to England. There wouldn't be anything from her now.

All those lives lost to the past, those personal interconnections that made who I became. What were those connections any more than stars visible from such a distance that they were already comatose if not stone-cold dead by the time their light touched me? True, nearly all elements in the human body were made in a star and many had come through supernovas. But none of that mattered, at the end of the day. It mattered even less when I was scrolled through life, when one minute I was there, the next I was here.

The bed was awfully comfortable.

"Good night, Green," said A I Green.

I was on the edge of sleep. Another reality, ill-defined. I'd never been able to predict the time jumps—what if they were nothing but dreams?

My eyelids flickered, fighting closure.

I wondered again what might happen if Zada *did* manage to arrest my movement way back in the past. Would I no longer be here, in the future? Would I be living in the present of a past life? Just like everyone else, and yet not.

It's a dream, it's not a dream, and it's floating me on an Oort cloud. I'm back in 1990 on the dance floor at the Sarah Sands, our bodies so close...Strobe lighting hits me, voltage...

Chapter 33

Green closes his eyes, sees the light through his eyelids. He doesn't care about anything other than Zada in his arms. This is what he's thinking as he feels himself splitting. He's here, where, not there.

And then blackness.

He comes to on his bum outside his parents' house. He stands and scratches his head.

The fog just happened?

Shouting, banging, yowls like those of a cat from inside the house tell him that his parents are at each other again. He sighs. His father is a man mountain, the bear. His mother the shrew who's trying to tame him.

Green rubs dust from his little boy shorts.

Then he sees the little girl about his age looking at him across the fence next door. She leaps over it and suddenly she's next to him.

"Are they always like that?" she asks.

He looks back at his house, the terrible sounds behind the door. "Pretty much."

"Mine too," she says. "Sometimes."

"You new around here?" he asks.

"Just moved from the Dandenong Ranges." She smiles, gap-toothed, and takes his hand. "My name is Zada."

Somewhere there
Someone other
on my mind

Zada

Chapter 1

2043

The house is an owl, jewel eyes unblinking, talons on ceilings. That's how she sees it, when it's not a waiting room, a vestibule that looks better from a distance. Or it's a gangway for a ship to nowhere, and it's not yet arrived to take her from here. The house is a stranger, too young to understand. It's not her house.

Zada steps over a scattered pair of sunnies, not hers. She pulls a comb through her thick black hair. When it tangles she swears. She's one of the few who still touches her hair. Others use wall bots to arrange, rearrange, fashion. She smiles—apparently years ago, there were hairdressers and someone other than a loved one would actually touch your hair!

She leans closer to the mirror. If she's going to keep the hair this jet black colour then she'll need to dye it again. It's already showing the dark gold in curly sprouts at the roots. She's unusual in this way, with the gold in her kinky hair, when it should be a natural black like her parents'. Perhaps that's why she dyes it now. But why black? To belong with her people? No. It's rebellion. No-one but Asante and Bakari, in their insistence on freethinking and communing with nature, leaves their hair natural any more. Everyone is wearing rainbows on their hair. When she looks in the mirror, she sees the fuchsia-haired guy sprawled across the waterbed. Gary, that's his name, another mistake. She could put it down to nerves at the forthcoming interview, at having headed out to the clubtrones and their retro music instead of staying at home, running through the questions she expects them to ask her at the interview. But really there are no excuses. Gary is a casual hook-up. She was there. He was there. That's all it needed to be. Same happened with Alan. Mo. Frida—she was a damn good kiss. A damn good everything, but for one night only.

Someday Zada would have to need more.

She's known from the onset that she is attracted to men. And women. She doesn't go looking for a gender to screw. Chemistry just happens. And with chemistry comes feeling, intense for a lifetime, but it lasts no more than days. She doesn't really care who ditches whom. Sometimes she leaves them hanging. Sometimes days pass and she realises, without astonishment, that they've left her hanging. Not that she's holding on. Maybe it's about saving face. Even if she doesn't care, it feels nicer doing the ditching rather than being dumped, right?

She looks at Gary, prone on his bed, comatose from yoga sex. She doesn't know whether to call it a wild thing, a straddle, backflip or something on the edge. His thighs were strong, that mattered. And their arms and knees seamlessly meshed. Now he has his arm over her empty pillow, same arm whose elbow had taken her to places at which she begged to linger, and he silenced her with ardent lips. Yet she's leaving, alone.

Sometimes she feels a longing for more, but what? Each time she casts an eye at the person asleep in the bed—she has chronic insomnia—she never feels a compulsion to stay. Her one nighters might have something to do with it, but sometimes she suspects she actually *wants* to be tied down to a singular relationship. She's a bit of a loner. And she prefers it that way.

There isn't much time to slip into a glider and head home and get changed. She finishes with her hair, throws the comb into her clutch purse. The door intuits her, pushes itself closed as if it knows she wants to use the toilet in privacy. She never gets it about those couples who pee doors open. Farts and burps are, for her, an intimacy breaker. She has affection for their source only when it's a bub, and that's about it. So Gary might have seen everything, yeah, yoga sex is as open as it gets, but he doesn't have to see *everything*.

She pulls out her tableau and scrolls through face after face absentmindedly. If she were alone, she might have pulled up a hologram, listened to their voice.

She realises that she's still putting off thinking about the interview. She wants that job with Safiri. She knows she's right for the role. She has the passion for it. Technology is always her forte. My prodigy, her father proudly told anyone who'd listen. As a toddler she was disassembling and reassembling her parents' automats before they even knew how to turn them on, let alone program them.

Chapter 2

The glider that delivers her from Blackburn to SocialBox in the central business district on Bourke Street has a metallic orange wave running across it. The megabuilding is an imposing structure that occupies what would generally take three office blocks.

She shows her wrist at eye level above the wobbling glass door, like molten silver, and it scans her. The door dissolves to let her in.

No-one is there to meet her.

She looks about the room shimmering with light, mirrors and polish everywhere in a yawning emptiness, except for a monstrous horned owl at the far end. She walks towards it but the owl gleams further away from her, and then it silhouettes and fades as if it were unreal.

"Hello," she says.

"Hello, lo, lo," her voice echoes, bouncing against wobbling walls.

"Would you like some tea?" an English voice startles her.

She swirls to nothing.

"Excuse me?" she says.

"My name is A I Green. We have been expecting you, Zada."

Walls dissolve and suddenly she's in what looks like a board room.

"Please, take a seat," says A I Green.

Zada is not sure which one to take—the room is too large. She walks to the far end, towards the head of the table, and the chair glides itself out for her. She sits and the chair glides back in.

She rests her hands on the table, and jumps, as right under her palms, unbeckoned, is a tablet.

She blinks at the contract, then looks at the room that feels alive everywhere.

"I don't understand," she says.

"There's nothing to understand, Zada. You have passed with flying colours."

"How? Don't you want to ask me questions?"

"A question is worded so as to elicit information," says A I Green. "We have all the information we want about you. Do *you* have questions?"

"Why, yes, I mean. When do I start?"

"Waste no time on rhetoric, you're here already. Do you want me to show you the lab?"

"Now?"

"Our quest is urgent, Zada."

"Don't I have to sign the contract? What if I say no?"

"But you won't. Remuneration is whatever you want. How would you like to head the Safiri Project on time travel?"

"Head?"

"The use of the word in this occurrence is not a noun relating to the upper part of the human body, Zada, but rather it is a verb pertaining to a leading position, by which we mean that you can assume the adjective of 'chief' or 'principal' to preface the word 'scientist' as a referent with respect to your role. Do you want the job, Zada?"

"I guess..." she says in a tone that implies acceptance, even though she's not quite sure what she's accepting.

"Is that a 'yes', Zada?"

"Yes," she says, more firmly.

"Good. Then our contract is signed. A copy is already in your tableau. Welcome to the Safiri Project, Zada. Now," says A I Green, and the tablet before her vanishes with its contract. The wall opposite Zada makes a gobbler sound, the kind you might hear when sinking mud is swallowing you. It then wobbles itself into a screen full of faces.

"We have researched and done background checks on potential candidates to work with you—all you need to do is pick the two or three you feel most connected with."

"Connected?"

"Our motto at SocialBox is the ultimate employee experience. Longevity is imperative in a time travel project that involves many years. Biologically, your vitals are good. Emotionally, not so good, Zada. But you have the skills that we need on this project. For mutual health and the success of a mutual quest, humans must create subjective feelings towards others if they are to forge a positively interlocked bond." A I Green pauses, as if listening to Zada's breathing. "We need you at your best, Zada."

"I don't know whether to be angry or elated," she says.

"Good," says A I Green. "It confirms our deduction of your emotional deficiency. We'll leave you for a moment with the holograms of each candidate in your shortlist, so they introduce themselves to you." •

Zada watches in half surprise and half amusement, as all faces bar four fade from the screen. "Let me get this clear— you've picked *my* shortlist?"

"According to your body language and the movements of your pupils, we were able to ascertain the degree of your chemistry with each individual. Take Sam, as a specimen... He looks to you like a potential bedmate, but you will not be sleeping with him, Zada, and you know that."

"Because?"

"Because is a subordinating conjunction, 'for the reason that', with two distinct forms, and your use of it forms an incomplete clause. See, Zada, your statistics show," a graph appears on the screen, "that your work ethics and keenness towards a tactical goal preclude you from having intercourse with a subordinate with whom you participate on a time-critical project."

"You know what, A I Green? I hope your calculations show that you're not in a position to fire me right now, because I suspect you need me. So get lost and let me pick my staff."

"Technically, the 1s and 0s in my binary encoding are there to ensure that I cannot 'get lost', Zada. It is also physically and virtually impossible for me to leave the room, let alone the building," says A I Green, "but for a few minutes I can turn on the background tasks feature that will allow my processor to ignore you."

Chapter 3

Zada is now home. She kicks her shoes off, rubs her neck. Who'd have guessed her day would be this eventful?

Good thing she'd gone clubtroning, she thinks, losing herself in retro beats, instead of prepping for an interview with a somewhat irksome AI that already knows her IQ, urinalysis, liver function, food predilection, emotional intelligence, how many eggs are in each ovary and at what point in time of her ovulation cycle, and everything about her universal proclivity towards individual men and women!

She holograms her mother, Asante, who Zada has always called by name.

"Hey Truffles." Asante's silhouette dances on air. She's wearing her characteristic hippy flow and a head wrap. "Did you fuck up the interview?"

"You know I wouldn't."

"Oh, I don't know. You're combustible," says Asante. "You self-destruct."

"Is that Precocious?" comes her father's voice from somewhere in the hologram. His head bobs for a moment alongside Asante's.

"I still love you, Bakari," Zada tells her father, in their customary greeting. "And I got the job."

Commotion on the holo, Zada's parents celebrating in their customary unconstrained way. Then Bakari, breathless: "You'll always leap to your dreams, Precocious. Even as a toddler you *took* what you wanted, discarded it to take something else."

"There was no taking in this interview, Bakari. If anyone was taking, it was them. They'd already onboarded me way before I showed up. I won't get bored with it, I promise."

After the holo, she contemplates her parents. She never knows what version she'll get: the organic life-ists who raised her in a simple bamboo bungalow with a vegetable garden and a loquat tree, when the rest of the world lived in mega multi-storeys mounting to the sky; the free-spiriters who might bounce on holo naked, her mother's tits hanging out (she's the one who taught Zada about yoga sex), her father not even wearing dick togs; the cryogenic-freeze crazed loons who insist on converting her into a religion whose altar is a facility with large tanks after tanks frozen with human remains for the ultimate resurrection of humankind.

Cryopreservation was once no less than a million dollars, but now it costs just five grand if you put a clause in your life insurance. Zada is not interested. She has gone through periods of teen rebellion where she refused to talk anything liquid nitrogen—now she can listen, it doesn't mean she has to do anything with what she's heard.

With Asante's coaxing, Zada has walked the accommodating phase of homeopathy and healthy eating—she did put her foot down at durian, whose soft, creamy fruit Asante would have sworn was manna from heaven. But the intensity of its aroma as the tree matured and its fruit ripened was too much, even for the local council, unable to withstand one more complaint from the neighbours, and they ordered the damn tree cut from the veggie patch in the backyard.

During show-and-tell at her different schools, Zada always found opportunity to revel fellow students with hologrammed presentations of her mother's garden: the fruit of the rambutan, sweet and white in its oval shape; light green lettuce, shiny and compact leafed, ready to eat raw or cooked; green peas full of spring, plump and popping out of their pods; crisp broccoli stalks pregnant with earthy florets still wet with dew. Zada would describe how to cook each food item, what it tasted like—whether it was succulent, tender, bitter, zesty, peppery or full of spice, and how so different each was from the multi-hued, cook-free cubes arrayed on supermarket trays.

For all her academics that jumped her from primary school to college, ensuring she was always the youngest and brightest in the class, Zada has always felt a "lacking". Despite her parents' pet names for her, Truffles, Precocious—and the ones like Explorer, Dreamer, Visitor and Daylight that never stuck—Asante and Bakari have their own ilk of unique affection towards each other that always seems to the exclusion of Zada. Daylight! If she is anywhere for them near daylight, it's secondhand. All her life she feels like she's following footsteps, stepping into another person's mould, feeling secondhand daylight. Her parents say that 'Visitor' is because she never stays long in the bungalow.

"In and out in a jiffy on your way to wandering," Asante tried to explain, but Zada just didn't get it. Visitor.

She once asked Asante and Bakari, perhaps also in association with the colour of her natural hair: "Am I adopted?"

That was the first and only time she ever saw them angry.

"*Adopted?*"

When Zada voiced the word, it was casual, innocent-like, but when it came out of her mother's mouth she realised how loaded it sounded. It wasn't just a word, it was an expression loaded with hurt.

Zada had stuck a finger into her curls and twisted, the tightness radiating a bud of pain that she offset against her mother's anger.

"Zada…" said her mother who almost never used her given name "…do you think we could have invested all this time in you if you weren't our own? Not that we wouldn't be caring and considerate to another child, but born from my own flesh… you've yet to have an idea of what that's like."

"It was a home birth too," said Bakari doggedly.

"Yes," affection in Asante's voice. "You remember those veggies in our garden, how they looked, how they tasted, how they *existed* differently from those cubed or manufactured things that you saw in the stores. It's a completely different calibration.

There's no comparison. Coming from me..." she looked at Bakari, "coming from *us*...is a wholly organic experience. And if you haven't *known* that, haven't *felt* that, then we must have done something wrong, something terribly wrong."

Bakari placed a hand on his wife's arm. "She knows we've given her our all, don't fret." He faced Zada. "Where is this coming from? This shot of rebellion."

Zada hunkered down. She didn't want this argument, she wanted validation of her parents' unequivocal love. Yet as a teenager she knew she couldn't accept her positioning versus that of the rest of the world, not at that age. She *had* to be anti-this, anti-that. It was hardwired into her DNA. And her parents had taught her to be a freethinker, had developed, even *conditioned*, her responses to such questioning. They had imbued in her the communist concept of agitprop, that intentional, vigorous promulgation of ideas. They had told her to question everything, to take nothing at face value, and yet, daring to question *them*, that was another matter. That was one step removed from their ideal.

At the time of the incident, her bringing up of adoption, and her parents' own interrogations of her that felt like curveballs launching towards her at speed, she didn't respond. She made a guttural, low-octave noise of frustrated aggression and turned on her heel. Then, despite chewing over everything during a night of increased shadows, she woke in the morning knowing they would have glossed over her outburst.

And, sure as rain, at the breakfast table it was as though nothing had happened. She didn't know what would have been worse: a simmering resentment that she had questioned their intentions or less assimilation of her outburst as being ultimately inconsequential. The fact they went with the latter suggested that, while she wasn't adopted, she might as well have been. She was an object for her parents to live their lives vicariously through.

They projected the best of themselves through Zada to facilitate her education, her life choices, her experiences, and… yes…that was great, but that channelling also left her a hollow vessel, unsure of who she might have been had she been left to her own devices. Unsure of who she—Zada—actually is today.

Now, sitting on her bed, massaging the soles of her feet, easing away the ache of the clubtrone experience, she understands that physical and emotional pain are two separate beasts. Her fingers might undo the knots in one, but her heart cannot totally ease the uncertainty of the other. Sure, her parents love her, but is love ever enough?

She considers her recent glut of casual relationships. Do they constitute freedom or the indiscriminate search for pleasure she can't find in a more stable environment? Her head begins to hurt.

She'll take a leaf from her parents' tree and focus on the future, because the future is bright and it's all she has.

Chapter 4

For all its remunerations, two years on and the Safiri Project is not a rosy one. Despite A I Green's shortlists and supercomputations of team bonding, the project is suffering from high staff turnover. People are moving on with alarming alacrity. Sam, her first employee pick, was the first to leave. A project that big is hard to keep secret, despite the confidentiality clause in the employment contract. A I Green seems to be on top of everything. He knows about leaks or intent to leak data, and quietly terminates contracts.

Problematic staff who go rogue and threaten to cause trouble if their services on the project terminate find themselves with cyber insecurities, identity crises, underpinning losses of credibility, let alone human existence, to an intensity that only an emotionless AI is capable of inflicting.

And A I Green is very capable.

One young woman who kicked up a bit of a fuss found herself extinct. In the literal sense. There was no record of her birth, schooling, marriage, mortgage, banking or simple existence. She was simply wiped off—even her own family wasn't sure about her any more. Then there was Ralph, who found himself a fugitive from the law, and nearly on death row in South America—that is, until he withdrew his intimidations against the project, and A I Green forgave enough to expunge Ralph's difficulties.

That is the measure of A I Green's capability. And the programming algorithms for the project too, that's a huge plus. At this point the experiments have moved way beyond transporting pencils, mugs and rats from Points A to Points Z in controlled environments.

Zada and her new scientist, Tula Bludge, have begun dimension testing on hogs that are the closest in DNA to the human body. But it's hard to send hogs back in time when they have no means of looping back a report. So in her mind Zada is of no doubt that, at some point, she'll just have to make herself a test subject.

When she mentions this to Tula, she finds herself surprised at the scientist's reaction.

"Now that's dedication to the cause!" Tula's eyes glitter in wonderment.

Not for the first time Zada finds herself attracted. Tula, in those sheer maxis, the silhouette of her body showing. Tula dresses less conservative than Zada. It's not surprising Zada's eyes trace the contours of Tula's skin that might ordinarily be hidden, reserved for the bedroom.

"How else would we know if any of this works?" asks Zada. "I'm tired of running programs for time-structural anomalies to see if some hog farmer pre-millennial reported a sudden surfeit of livestock. We know we've got the means to make stuff disappear, but where and when to, and does it remain alive? How're we ever going to answer those questions without hitching a ride ourselves?"

"But you'd take that risk?" Tula looks around. Zada imagines she's considering A I Green in this conversation, perhaps wondering whether questioning Zada's motives might get her the shove.

"We're talking hypothetically, right?" Zada says louder than she needs to, hoping Tula will catch on. "We're both dedicated to the cause, we're just chatting over the best way to achieve it."

Tula nods. Thoughtful. "Only if something sentient goes back will we know if we can go forwards. I know this. Ain't no hog going to be pressing any buttons on our prototype."

"Yet we know that going forward is a possibility." Zada is referring to their knowledge of Green, the version that A I Green is modelled on. Green is the only reason the Safiri Project exists. A retro podcast, Jumping Time, is at the heart of their efforts. But how much can she trust A I Green?

Zada suspects A I Green is drip-feeding information. What she does know is that Green has been moving forwards in time faster than should be humanly possible. She has the proof of his existence uploaded on her tableau. Records of his date of birth, his parentage, early upbringing. But then interactions with governmental departments go haywire. He goes off the map for long periods of time that even in those days should be accounted for. If everyone leaves a footprint, then Green is stomping with giant steps.

But, Zada wonders—she has always wondered—if it came down to the age-old question. If time jumping is possible, then where are all the other time jumpers?

It aggrieves her that A I Green has denied her access to certain project data. That she's working from limited information based on A I Green's "need to know" calculus. She's almost certain that A I Green has ulterior motives, that he's keeping stuff from her, for reasons that Zada hopes are not tied into the Safiri Project's stated goals (that would beat the project's very purpose, Zada's whole purpose in it) or are illegal. She doesn't want to find herself in a mushroom farm for penance.

Of course, she's aware A I Green is modelled on Green. Hence the name, right? But other than understanding SocialBox is funded through investments Green made in the past, she's not totally sure of the connection between them. And who knows what a rogue AI can get up to? She has no certainty of his rogueness, but he certainly *is capable* of much. The fact that A I Green can be here without Green worries her slightly. But not enough to think about it too hard.

"So," Tula continues, "you would take that risk?"

"My desire to *know* is burning a big, bright hole. Isn't yours?"

"Right up the point of my personal safety."

Zada nods. Earlier experiments fritzed hogs on the spot. She wonders often about purpose. She can go back in time to do *what*? Fuck everything up for the future? She knows it's an old story, almost folklore by now, but there is that tiny detail called the Butterfly Effect. However much in theory it has been disproved.

A I Green downloaded a paper onto her tableau regarding the research two theoretical physicists—Nikolai Sinitsyn and Bin Yan—had done at the Los Alamos National Laboratory over 20 years ago. Using a quantum computer to simulate time travel they'd discovered that, in the quantum realm at least, there was no butterfly effect. In their research, information—qubits, or quantum bits—"time travelled" into the simulated past. One of the quantum bits was then strongly damaged, but surprisingly, when all qubits returned to the "present", they appeared largely unaltered, as if reality was self-healing.

Sinitsyn confirmed that, on a quantum computer, there was no problem simulating opposite-in-time evolution, or simulating a process that ran backwards into the past and, from that basis, could actually see what happened with a complex quantum world if we travel back in time, add small damage, and return. They found that their "world" survived, meaning there was no butterfly effect in quantum mechanics.

Of course, simulation and reality are different beasts. And that recent paper isn't much younger than her. Zada wonders what other experiments might be happening—right around the world—which were just as secret as those at Safiri.

Green—though—Green is their key.

"So," Zada says, wanting to deflect the negative aspects of the conversation, "if you could go back—and return to our present—where would you travel to?"

Tula places her elbows on the desk pointing upwards, hands clasped with her chin resting on them, pyramid-like. "Would you believe I haven't given it much thought? What about you?"

"I'd be interested in seeing the world before flying cars and sex robots existed. Maybe check out why the dinosaurs really became extinct."

Tula laughs. She knows Zada is paraphrasing historical stereotypes. "Me," Tula adds, "maybe I'd return to watch my parents meet for the very first time. Be there at that moment when they realise they're in love."

Now it's Zada's turn to laugh: "I had no idea you were such a romantic."

"But don't you think it would be amazing? You know that old saying, about the moment you were only a twinkle in your daddy's eye. Wouldn't it be incredible to view the first moment of your existence?"

"Sounds to me you want to watch your parents having sex!" Zada laughs louder, not quite sure what she's laughing for. Perhaps it's fear because it occurs to her suddenly: what if Tula is a soulmate?

She's never thought this of anyone, let alone someone in her staff. But it's now 2045, two years into the project, and Tula is the one person she feels most connected with. Zada's relationship with Tula would merit A I Green's probability calculus on "a positively interlocked bond". Tula is the one person most aligned in qualities and dedication to Zada. Like Zada, she gives herself, empties herself in a moment, in every crucial moment.

"Am I right, or am I right?" teases Zada.

Tula pulls a face. "Parents and sex are two subjects I prefer not to speak of in the same sentence, irrespective of verb or adjective." She holds Zada's gaze. "But you know what I mean. Wouldn't that work for you — seeing your exact formation, that precise moment of your existence?"

Zada wonders. She wonders *exactly* what she might see in her parents' faces as they contemplate giving her life. Maybe she *wouldn't* see that twinkle of loneliness that she can never shift, that has always been there.

"Come on," she says, "let's go eat."

SocialBox has been developing food capsules. Part of the company's income is derived from supplying space stations and modern restaurants trending on cubes and pills. But Zada wants real food in her belly, no matter how nutritionally satisfying those capsules might be.

"Wait, really." Tula hurries after Zada. "Let's talk this... jumping back in time with you in it?"

Chapter 5

A I Green summons Zada into the board room and seals it.

"Zada, you wouldn't," he says.

"Wouldn't what, A I Green? I thought you knew all about hanging or subordinate clauses."

"Have sexual intercourse with Tula."

Zada is stunned into silence. Then she laughs. "Easy, A I Green. It was just lunch. Wasn't it you who reasoned that, based on my statistical data on work ethics and keenness towards a tactical goal, it was impossible for me to sleep with someone who is working for me?"

"You, Zada, are an anomaly."

"Something tells me you didn't summon me here to discuss sex or anomalies. Shoot."

"A shoot is a bud when it is a noun, but the verb pertains to a discharge of—"

"Just show me why I'm here, A I Green."

The furthest wall wobbles and morphs itself into a screen display of holographic projections. A minimal scatter of points intersects, then lines appear to connect with the dots and they form a square. The square fades out, grows larger and more dimensional to transition into a cube, then a cube-in-a-cube that silhouettes into a 4D-cube fading in and out of the screen, now and then bouncing from one end to the other.

"Well?" says Zada.

"This is a hypercube, also known as a Tesseract," says A I Green. "I want to talk to you about dimension theory."

It dawns on Zada. "A Tesseract uses time as a dimension…"

"Yes. I think we're onto a winner. It's not just a travelling device—it could reset Green's jumps into the future and help stabilise them. But it will take at least two years to perfect a working prototype," says A I Green. "During which time, I want you to prepare for time jumping."

"You want to send me back to the past?"

"You want that."

"How would you know, A I Green?"

"Your conversation with Tula—"

"Tssk! You been eavesdropping."

Silence. Then: "You have the IQ, passion and survival skill to do it, let alone your capacity to lead, mentor and communicate."

"Sure, but..." She thinks about it. "Will I need training like an astronaut? You know—practise how to fit into a spacecraft or something like that? Full-blown military land and sea survival tactics and all that fun?"

"Time travel is a different kind of training, Zada. You'll need to decondition your mind and body."

"I guess you're not talking scuba diving, weightlessness and the coolest shit. See, I don't know anything about orbital dynamics."

"You don't need to understand orbital dynamics. What you need, Zada, is to assimilate the cultures and mindsets of decades earlier. You need to tone your language—"

"For example?"

"For example, Zada, you can't blurt about artificial intelligence and supercomputing to a shop attendant in the 1990s."

"They might burn me on a stake?"

"Death by burning is an execution method—"

"A I Green, I'm only joking."

"A joke is something one says to cause amusement, but our discussion, Zada, does not warrant a punchline."

"Ease up, Broomstick, I'm listening. Anything else I need to know?"

"Zada, you'll need to understand the differences in social etiquette across decades. Women in the past are more—"

"Demure?"

"The further back you go—"

"The tighter I'll need to keep my legs closed? I've never felt more insulted."

"An insult is scorn or abuse, and in medical terms it is an event that causes damage to a tissue or an organ."

"Aha! Right there, A I Green! Now we're getting closer to the important things you might be omitting. Let's talk for a minute about injuries—what are my chances of surviving a time jump?"

"Your vitals are exceptionally healthy, and we can condition you with emotional intelligence implants—"

"Fuck that, A I Green. I'm not a child."

"No, Zada. You're not a newborn, toddler or juvenile but you're the offspring of your parents, which does make you a child, nee."

"Can we just...?"

"What you need is John Roc on your staff." The image of a man shows on screen. "He has a PhD in past civilisations. I have prepared his employment contract and have already set up a meeting."

Zada frowns at the contract on the screen. "It says Chief Information Officer."

"Information, yes. He'll teach you time endurance, what people eat, how people talk across eras you'll time jump into. You will need to know the slang and lingo across different timelines."

"Why?"

"There are significant socio-economic differences—"

"Such as?"

"Banking—people use ATMs and EFTPOS in the past and, further back, you must walk into a bank and carry a paper bank book. Don't worry—I can give you access to Green's accounts. You'll need to learn basic first aid, bushcraft, hand-to-hand combat to thwart a would-be rapist or pickpocket. You will need the right clothing, shelter, food and navigation."

"Anything else, A I Green? I am trying not to be cynical."

"There's no time for sarcasm. You have only two years to get ready, Zada. And John is on his way in now."

Chapter 6

John Roc is a good-looker. He's very tall and very bald. He is personable, even in his handshake—he wraps her in a cushy glove that is a big warm hand, and it puts her at ease. Until he opens his mouth.

"A I Green says that you're completely uncultured to the past."

"Is this how you make a good impression at an interview?"

"A I Green says—"

"We might get on a better footing without paraphrasing what A I Green says. I want to know about you, John. Somehow you make me feel judged."

"Sounds like you want to know about you, Zada. And I'm not judging you. What you'll get from me is candidness, not judgement. You don't strike me as one who's looking for a yes-man to pamper and mislead you into history."

She glares at him for a moment, uncertain whether to like him or dislike him, then she laughs. He grins back, something wholesome, earnest. He's raw. Unique. He smells of wood and lemon, she wonders what he's wearing. "I think I like you," she says.

"That's a good start."

"I think Tula will like you too."

"Tula?"

The board room wall wobbles and fades to show a mirror of Tula tinkering with a cubed device in the lab.

Zada's mood brightens considerably. "A I Green doesn't waste time," she says. "And he certainly wants our positive subjective feelings towards each other. His own words, I swear. Come—I'll introduce you to the rest of the team."

He follows her out of the board room. "Is it a big team?"

"There's me. There's A I Green who you've already met."

"I am here, Zada," says A I Green.

"You always are. Are you doing this tour or am I?" She steers John into the lab. "And that there's Tula, our chief scientist." She gestures at him. "And now there's you, John."

"And he has homework for you," A I Green speaks from the lab.

"Anything Tesseract, please," says Zada.

"Actually," says John. There's a timbre in his voice that Zada likes. "Australia has a troubling past—you'll do well to understand cultural aspects associated with the white invasion, penal settlements, citizenship and immigration policies."

"Sure thing."

"And food. It might take time to acclimatise to a different diet. Go easy on new stuff. Food-related disorders come in all shapes, and the people in the past might not know how to handle your evolved body."

"Oh?"

"You want to avoid accident or injury, hospitals, diseases. Anything where you'll be under close scrutiny."

"That's scary. I don't want to end up in a top security government lab."

"No. You also need to know that there was the COVID-19 pandemic. There were a few causes of panic across the years, but this one rattled the world more than a little. You want to avoid jumping into any time between 2019 and 2023."

"I thought our genes mutated for better immunity."

"Viruses mutate faster—it's those older ones we need to worry about more." He looks at her. "Now, Australia also has a rich history of premiers, prime ministers, political turntables, footy stars, floods, bushfires and a host of award-winning actors and actresses."

"Okay…" Zada says hesitantly. "Doesn't sound very techy."

"Trivia has a way of catching up on you in the past," says John.

"They even have a name for it—Trivial Pursuit," says A I Green. "Everywhere, into the 2020s, people play bingo and trivial pursuit, garbling nonsense at each other for money or as conversational icebreakers."

"A I Green has downloaded for you an archive of the 1990s, 2000s, 2010s, 2020s through now," says John.

"I hope there's something in those archives about clubtrones."

"In the past, you go clubbing, not clubtroning. A I Green has also particularly asked me to discuss with you about..." He hesitates, looks around the room, but Tula is busy, and A I Green has gone silent. "To discuss with you about murders in Bondi Beach in the event that you gallivant from Melbourne into Sydney. That was in the 80s—there was a lot of gay hate. But, what do you know, things changed quickly, and same-sex marriage became legal in 2017."

Tula walks up to them. She's in a bodice mesh suit: a breast-cup number, sheer tie-front skirt with a big belt—it's see-through, her long legs going all the way to super-high heels. "I heard we're getting a new starter. And you're already talking sex." She accepts John's handshake. "I knew Zada was fast..."

"I'm not that fast."

"We make an ace team," says Tula. A wink at Zada.

Chapter 7

Zada looks out of the window. Her city is a megamodel pregnant with decorations. It's filled with figures moving, nothing she wants close. She wants to escape the city. But she is the city.

Now she's a narrow road, all around hedges gobbling air. Now she's a story at night, blinking on the screen. She's a finger groping, searching for a signal. She's a stocking, why are her feet so cold? Her cheek is prickling. What she wants, what she really wants are wings that will fly her away. But warm hands are exploring her eyelids, her cheek, the corner of her mouth, her chin.

Zada wakes up in a curl, hugging the pillow. The dream about Tula envelops her still. The curves inside Tula's sheer lover sarongs. Those mesh maxi dresses that cone her breasts in silhouette, yet soft to cup, don't belong in the office. But Zada will be damned if she'll have a word. She pushes her mind off Tula's inner belly button, not an outer one like Zada's, off the voluptuous hips and long, long legs, off the possibilities of their kiss: full of berries and mint.

Zada dyes her hair jet black, then showers. She makes coffee. Yesterday with John went rather well, far more than she anticipated. Her determination to frustrate A I Green, if that were even possible, by rejecting his candidate, melted as soon as John opened his mouth and started walking her through the past. He, like A I Green, is capable. In her mother's words, he can organise more than a chook raffle.

From the lab they wound up next door at Je Taime, a patisserie brimming with classic croissants, canelés, vanilla centres and caramelised crusts, almond and coffee-drenched ganaches, macarons and whatnots. Zada helped herself to an almond macaron filled with buttercream ganache, having weighed it against a delightful praline pastry. John watched her with amusement, and allowed Zada to tempt him into a flan pâtissier that oozed custard. Tula would take no more than a bite of an éclair.

The coffee came in shots of espresso, bitter, a little smoky, a chocolate and nut finish on the tongue. Certainly kept Zada up a bit, took her a while to find sleep. Now she stretches and climbs out of bed. Her flat in Carlton, off the corner of Elgin and Lygon Street, is pre-modern. It came with a sizzler shower and a stone bench kitchen—none of those bot-manned apartments. But she does have a robot vacuum that infolds into tiny places to gobble dirt.

She generally grabs groceries from Naturo Store on Johnston Street near the Green Man's Arms. There's another natural food store just after The Wine Corner in Brunswick where they sell health food, but a tiny portion of it, be it beans or cheese, costs a liver and two kidneys. Sometimes, like last night, she orders meals in non-cubed, non-pilled takeaway.

She smiles to herself. She found her teeth on rabbit food and meals tossed with fruit and nuts. Bakari said peanut oil kept the brain alive and maybe that accounts for Zada's precocity and vigorous metabolism, but she'll swear to anybody who listens that she'll never ram a tablespoon of hand-pressed vegetable oil down her child's, *any child's*, throat like her parents did to her.

She pops to work briefly, avoids Tula. John's not formally started yet. Zada decides on a detour. She takes a company glider to the Dandenong Ranges and manoeuvres it to a standstill on a mound of green between towering trees.

Her parents live in an eclectic village on a caveman diet up on the Dandenong Ranges away from city bustle where they can go full ape on nature. Their world is surrounded by rhododendrons—giant in pink, and lilac bells in spring, camellias—overlapping in white, variegation or blush hues in summer, daffodils in their sunlight yellow and cool autumn notes in a nose language that sometimes speaks hyacinth, jasmine or oriental.

When Asante and Bakari aren't gobbling bananas, durian, coconut meat, leaves and occasional bugs that are rich in protein, healthy fats, iron and calcium, but low in carbohydrates, they are looping through fern glades and forest vistas spectral in colours of the rainbow or demure in a soft mountain mist. Sometimes, but rarely, their world is dusted in winter snow, of which Zada has fond memories—putting her tongue out to taste the fresh, cool melt.

Asante loves hand-picking berries that grow fat and wild in the bush. Bakari takes to glassware jewellery that he sells in a boutique in Sassafras, just near the Koala Walk and the ten thousand steps that tourists from the city like to exercise on.

Zada doesn't visit here much because it can get awkward. She knows her parents feel comfortable in their bodies, and how most of the eclectic village is a hammock-strung nudie zone sprawling with fern gullies, temperate rainforest trees and the moon ash eucalypt.

From when she was a toddler, Zada manoeuvred escape from her parents, lifting the latch in her playpen and pushing a chair to the door so she could turn its handle. Before freedom, she had one giant step down, so she shuffled backwards on her hands and belly, feet feeling for the ground until she could stand, and then run.

She carries stubborn memories of nature, her penchant for stroking the bark of trees, dipping into streams, listening to the air and finding lacunas—any space or gap in which she could hide from Asante and Bakari.

Her parents taught Zada to be outdoorsy and she grew strong hiking legs. "Sturdy as a mule," Bakari affectionately said of her.

Growing up in the hilly ranges in a hippy commune, she both loved and hated it when her father cycled her to and from school, perching her in a hand-woven sisal basket appended to an old mountain bike that sighed and groaned.

She wore hand-sewn bibbed pinafores and smocking dresses, nothing like the metallic shimmer bodysuits—temperature controlled, health monitoring—that she discovered "normal" kids in her class wore.

She watched as the other children soared to the school grounds in sonic-gliders, and they looked at her bare-chested father, his unbuttoned jacket sweeping in the wind and slapping at her face, his bell-bottomed legs giving good grunt on the pedal.

These were the same children who—unlike healthy-as-a-mule Zada—suffered from grass and pollen allergies when they went on excursions down the Great Ocean Road, and walked nature trails. They snorted and sneezed like banshees, some of them coming out in fierce hives. They whimpered on dust tracks, squealed rather than marvelled at possums. One fell in fits at the sight of a joey in its mother wallaby's pouch.

Asante had no respect for those children's mothers: "Couldn't organise a chook raffle," she would say. That's where Zada got the phrase.

It didn't stop her shame at her father's bike whose parts (tyres, brakes, chain rings, seats) he made himself or improvised to closest fit: there was once a mouth-blown cow horn for a bell, and it mortified her when he used it as he swerved a landing glider.

She consoled herself that, at least, she wasn't plodding along on a reined donkey as she'd seen another mother in the commune do.

Now, as she approaches the bungalow and its black bamboo, she worries about how she might broach the topic of her time jumps. Doesn't matter that it's a couple of years away. She's not sure Asante and Bakari, with their cryogenics and all, will understand. Worse if she tells them it might be a one-way trip, no coming back.

Chapter 8

Two children run out squealing into her path, both as naked as the day they entered the world. A boy and a girl. They swerve round her, squeals reduced to chuckles. The girl has a stick with a purple flower bud burgeoning at the tip. They glance at Zada as though her clothes are the anomaly, then scoot round the back of the property, their motion soon lost, their noise becoming muted. They are not only a reminder of herself, but an emblem of the disconnect between the life here and the life in the city. And both those lives will disconnect with the life she might be heading into the past for. What life? At this stage, she doesn't know.

She's lived here—then why is she edgy? Sometimes she scares herself in echoes. It's as if the world talks back at her. She grew up here but doesn't belong here. She's the landscape. She's the woods. What she really wants is to stand at a window, to look out at a garden, and feel that she's here, not in colour or texture, just truly *here*. Not a mask, never worn. Not a stain, featureless. Not a shuffle, unfamiliar. Perhaps a beginning to an end. A dream inside a beating heart.

"Hey Truffles." Asante has come out onto the stoop. "Why didn't you tell us you were visiting?"

Because I didn't want speculation on the reason why, thinks Zada. *Because to tell you this I want to come in fresh.*

"Reasons," she says, as though she's a recalcitrant teenager again. She steps up and embraces her mother, who air-kisses inches away from her cheeks.

"Well, don't just stand there. C'mon in."

It's been a while since Zada has physically walked into her old home. The holovids—her parents' in-between to balance nature and modernity—don't offer any kind of connection and, anyway, her parents often change the background vista to suit their moods, not Zada's.

She isn't surprised to see that little has changed. The same wooden table, scoured with age. The same chairs with the mis-lengthened legs, those her father carved for the glee of creation, without care for measurement. To be authentic, to be rustic, he'd said, even though every time they sat, they rocked from side to side on the slate-tiled floor. The pan bubbling away on the hob even pre-dated her birth. It was the best pan for rice-cooking, Asante had insisted, when Zada offered to buy something more modern as an anniversary gift. The smell of the rice was a familiar comfort: that warm, fluffy scent that gave this home a real sense of *home*.

"Bakari's at the store," Asante says, pulling out one of the chairs. "So, what have we done to deserve this pleasure?"

Zada can't tell her mother without her father present. It will be difficult enough saying it once, not also a second time with Asante chipping in every third word.

"It can wait."

"Well, let me fix you up a bowl of fruit."

Asante stands again and goes to the fridge. She pulls out a tub of natural yoghurt. At the counter, Zada watches as Asante deftly peels the skin from rambutans and lychees, takes a paring knife and denudes a mango, the flesh dripping with orange goodness, before throwing some black grapes into a bowl. She adds the rest of the fruit and pours homemade yoghurt over the top. "Here you go."

Zada sits. Rocks. The flavours explode in her mouth. As though she has synaesthesia she sees colours in her mind, a cornucopia of abundance. The slight sour tang of the yoghurt, the sweetness of the fruit, the honeyed, aromatic taste of the lychees, in particular. She's only on her fourth heaped spoonful before she sees Asante glance at the door and a shadow falls over her bowl. She knows Bakari has entered behind her.

"Precocious!" he shouts. Then he wraps his arms around her from behind, pinning her to the chair. She smells the turning of cut wood, the vague meaty smell of his skin, the hairs on his forearms raising goosebumps on hers. After the hug, he pulls out a chair opposite, Asante to his left. Zada suddenly senses a shift in the dynamic. They understand she is here for a reason. Their positions indicate those of a job interview.

"So, what do we owe the pleasure?"

Asante digs him with her elbow. "That's exactly what I said."

Zada runs her spoon around the inside of the bowl, clearing the last of the yoghurt and flecks of fruit. She takes a breath.

"I have some news, regarding my job. I might…I might be going away for a while."

"A trip!" Bakari claps his hands together, delighted. "They say travel broadens the mind and I'd never disagree. New places, new cultures, it all aids to a global understanding."

"Don't get too excited, Bakari," Asante says, her hand moving to his elbow. "Whereabouts are you going?"

Zada sidesteps the question. "Still in Australia, only…" she wonders how A I Green will feel about her spilling the beans on her work. She wonders if—even here—there's a way for him to listen in. She has authorisation to inform her parents about the trip. A I Green doesn't want them to report her as missing, after all, but there are limits.

Zada isn't sure what scares her most, her parents' likely reaction or trying to get them to sign the required confidentiality agreement once they've heard the news. "Only…not in the way you might think." She pushes the empty bowl into the middle of the table. She tells them about her research, the successes so far with the hogs, the next step.

"Into the past?" Asante says, disbelieving.

"Make sure you come and visit," Bakari laughs. "You can see just what a handful you were as a teenager!"

They aren't taking her seriously.

"I'm going away into the past." Zada repeats her words to them, slowly, hoping they are listening, truly listening.

Realisation clouds their eyes. For once, their jocularity is threatened. Zada realises this trailblazing is *exactly* what they wanted for her, their daughter, and yet the reality of it is something else.

"Is this actually possible?" says Bakari, taking a more sustained interest. "To travel to the..." He leaves the difficult words hanging.

"The technology will be there. Two, three years at most. It's a headfuck, I know, but people say that about almost every technological advancement. When you guys were young, supercomputers were in their infancy."

Bakari nods. "Something straight out of science fiction," he muses, then begins a monologue about having read HG Wells, Asimov, Jemisin and Octavia Butler.

"I have recurring dreams of travelling to other planets, of humankind putting aside disagreements for the common good, of serious scientific advances that progress with an eye on environmentalism and are ethically appropriate."

As Zada tolerates the speech, she watches Asante. The vibe from both parents is that they were pre-prepared, as though they held an expectation of this.

"Like journeying to Mars," Asante says. "We did wonder— many years ago, when you were growing up—if going to Mars might be your destiny."

"That ship's already left," Bakari says. "And that's a one-way trip..." He catches the look in Zada's eyes. "Just how long are you going to be away?"

Zada realises she's biting on her right forefinger, her teeth leaving tiny indents in the skin. "It's not yet decided," she says. Then goes for a half-truth. "The technology isn't quite there yet to bring me back."

Asante stands. She picks up the empty bowl. The spoon clatters around the inside like a motorbike rider around the wall of death. Taking it to the sink she rinses it thoroughly and parks it on the draining board. Turning around, she leans backwards against the work surface.

"Can you contact us while you're away?"

Zada shakes her head.

"So this is like...goodbye?"

Zada is astonished to see tears at the edges of her mother's eyes. Yes, they've always been supportive, yes, they've been loving and kind, but distance has also always been there... She wonders if Asante is sad for Zada's leaving with no understanding of return, or sad for her own self and a possible sense of loss.

"At least two more years till I go," Zada says. "You've still got me." She stands and embraces Asante, feels her bony structure within the loose material of the hippy flow. Just as she's on the point of crying herself, she realises Asante is no longer crying.

Bakari takes his time to rise and walk over. Then embraces them both. Zada feels the warmth radiate. Despite never being totally sure of her family's emotions—even when they're so apparently worn on their sleeves—the group hug is animal. It's a panther or a leopard, keen and wild. It's a lioness, the smell of her musky coat enough to carry as a memory. Even if Zada never sees Asante and Bakari again, at least she will have this.

Chapter 9

"Are you ready?" Tula asks her.

"As I'll never be. Two years I've been getting ready."

She's been doing laps of work, bouncing off walls.

Tula smiles wide. "You can still joke about this, Zada. It gives me such relief to see you this calm."

"Ah, I'm thinking you're just relieved it's not you doing the journey."

"No, Zada. You know that's not it." There's deep affection in her voice. "I would have stayed over even if A I Green hadn't asked me to."

"I reckon he'll be very surprised that…"

"Nothing happened?" says Tula.

Zada laughs. "Yes, he says I'm an anomaly."

Zada is grateful that Tula stayed the night. They slept together on her bed, facing each other, untouching, at ease. A platonic arrangement that A I Green suggested, knowing Zada needed the emotional stability and support to embark upon her mission.

During the last couple of years, Zada realised she was A I Green's preferred "specimen"—his exact wording, for the time jumps—because he identified her flawed familial and relationship ties. She would head into a past of no return because she had such little investment in the future. Acknowledging this was a suck but, despite Zada's faint protestations, and they were rather faint, he knew she would come around. It still needed explaining, and A I Green was brutal in his choice of words— "feeble familial construction", "arbitrary sleep-arounds", "uninvested actuality"—so that she realised there was nothing to cling to.

Even so, saying goodbye to Tula, to her parents, to A I Green, to John…isn't easy.

They take a sonic-glider. Zada looks out at a city which will become futuristic to her in a matter of a few hours once she enters the past. There are definitely things she'll miss—the clubtrones for one thing, and—if John is correct—the instances of casual yoga sex, casual being the key word. But the past has become as exciting to her as the future is for anyone in the present. The past is literally her future. She has the best of both worlds.

Tula's fingers have snaked familiarly into hers, their legs pushed together inside the glider.

"You purr in your sleep," says Zada.

"I do not!"

"You do too."

"Is that why you didn't...?"

"There are many reasons why I 'didn't', Tula, and I'm taking them all with me to the past." She squeezes Tula's hand. "And I've seen how you look at John."

"You have not!"

Tula lays her head on Zada's shoulder.

They maintain this frisson for the length of the journey, Zada wondering if both their minds are on what-could-have-beens and—if the return journey becomes a possibility—what still-might-be should they be successful.

Zada has made half-a-dozen trips so far. A controlled experiment. The first was for a few seconds. Within the depths of a laboratory, Tula placed a glass of water on a pedestal. Zada downed the water in one, pressed the Tesseract, and found herself newly standing before a full glass of water once more, undrunk. The second experiment was riskier. Zada spent an hour within a locked room, performing various physical and psychological tasks and then re-performing them once the jump happened. Initially, she felt woozy after each jump, at first up to a week of being unsteady on her feet. As Tula and A I Green refined the Tesseract, the blackouts were less fierce, and Zada's recovery picked up to days, then hours, and finally, minutes.

The memory loss is temporal, and she still worries what will happen if she forgets her entire past/future in a jump.

There's still no technology to bring her back to the future, so she has to readjust in real time. This is why the experiments cannot send her back much further. She cannot disconnect too much with the present reality. Besides, as A I Green says over and over, time is only a nonspatial continuum that's measured in terms of events that succeed one another from past through present to future. Going back in time simply rearranges the order of those events for the individual traveller. If it is effective for one second, or an hour, then it will be effective for a year, for 10 years, for a millennium. It is only how she then rearranges those events in her head on arrival that's important. She mustn't lose herself in the potential complexity of it.

Their fingers disengage as Zada and Tula reach SocialBox. The side doors of the glider rise upwards and Zada and Tula step out onto the street. The sky is a pale blue, summer is coming. Across from the building, galahs commingle on eucalyptus branches, native trees still permeating the sidewalks of a megacity. At least Zada has that to look forward to. The wildlife will remain the same.

Zada had felt no serious ill-effects after her recent jumps. One moment she was here and the next she was there in exactly the same space. A I Green has explained there will be subtle changes when she goes further back. The Tesseract has a sensor that accounts for the Earth's movement, so she won't suddenly appear on the other side of the world, in the heart of a jungle, the core of a volcanic mount or the middle of the ocean. Unlike Green's jumps, which from his podcast Zada knows are involuntary, she does have a measure of control over dates, times and locations. Yet, as with all technology, inevitably there is a substantial measure of the unknown. She will only know how precise her jumps are once she makes them. She shoves this uncertainty back deep into the pit of her stomach.

"C'mon," says Tula. Her voice is shaking as much as her legs in her ridiculously high heels. "Let's go in."

Zada realises that when she comes out, the building she is entering won't even exist.

John is waiting in the foyer.

"Ready?" His bald head is shiny in the gleam of SocialBox lights.

"I better be." Zada's trust in him has grown over their time together. John has been A I Green's best gift to her.

John takes her hand. "Zada, are you sure about this? It's only a prototype, remember. Who knows precisely how interdimensional travel works? We don't know how the past and present regroup in time warp. Your whole past or future could become anomalous."

"A I Green says I already am an anomaly."

"Causal effects or not, and all that—think about it. Resetting the Tesseract might shift you into a multiverse. A whole new instance of you."

"Seen my childhood? That would be nice."

He shakes his head. "I wish you'd take this more seriously."

"But I am."

"Well, then. So your first jump is to 2028. We know, from Jumping Time, that Green was there, and was planning to meet someone at Je Taime. I wish he were more specific about where he was staying, and we have 17 July as a close timeline from his 'Hey mate, what's the date?' thing he did on SocialBox vids."

"But we don't know if the Tesseract allows exactitude in months," explains A I Green.

"You could arrive in June or August," says Tula.

"So perhaps it's best that I set my jump to land about May?" says Zada. "It will give me a few months to find Green before his own uncontrolled time jumps."

"We have a plan," agrees John.

"The time is now?" Zada hesitates.

John takes her hand briefly. His touch is calming. "You'll be right. The time is now. We'd better give you space lest you bring us with you to the past." He smiles, hugs her.

She clings to his wood and lemon smell, then clutches Tula to her chest even longer.

"A I Green, even though you've hid stuff from me, you're my pal."

"A pal is a close associate, a chum or a comrade," says A I Green in monotone. "John and Tula, you will observe that I have been palled. Zada, we'll be pals for a long time. That means indefinite, continued existence. Let the records state that I like pal-ling."

Zada takes the Tesseract from her clutch purse and sets it. Her eyes are stinging with the unshed tears her parents have taught her.

She stands away from them and triggers the Tesseract.

Chapter 10

Zada blinks. She feels lost. It takes her a few minutes to recognise her surroundings. She's standing on Bourke Street right where SocialBox once stood. In its place are office blocks and shopfronts. She looks at the fitted clothes shop and then Je Taime right opposite. There are no gliders in sight. A Rolls Royce shuttle drives past.

She crosses the road to familiarity that is also strangeness, like the woman with a scarf at the counter, who greets her with, "You want crumpet? Is good. Half price."

"Just an espresso, please."

"Three dollars fifty," the woman says. "No mille-feuille? Is good. I make six dollars all."

"Yeah," says Zada, "okay." She's worried. A I Green said the Tesseract would work. A multipurpose time wizard. Despite real-time experiments in the future, what if it doesn't work on this timeline?

The woman types into the keypad of a device and pushes it toward Zada.

Zada hesitates. Then takes out the Tesseract and hovers it above the machine. To her astonishment, the device beeps and accepts payment. It prints out a receipt.

Zada is relieved. She'd started contemplating sweeping floors, washing dishes, to make up for money she couldn't pay. She has no skills, credentials, papers to work in this world. Even if she somehow got hold of her birth certificate or passport, no-one would believe her. Anything from the future would appear very forged and extremely incredible.

She looks at the date on the receipt. A I Green was right about the Tesseract's time specificity. It's not May. She doesn't have a few months to find Green. It's July, and shit! It's 17 July 2028.

"Is different bank, no?" The woman points at the Tesseract.

"Yeah. NAB," says Zada quickly, and puts the Tesseract away.

She mulls over her options over coffee, asks as she leaves, "Is there a place I can stay around here? A hotel maybe?"

"*Beaucoup d'hôtels par ici.* The Diplomat three-star. *C'est le meilleur.* The best." She gives directions.

Chapter 11

For a 3-star hotel, the Diplomat is something else. Zada walks past a pink lake, flamingos wading in it. Rosy galahs eye her from the eucalyptus trees lining the walkway to the reception, where a young waitress offers her a cocktail with smoke coming out of it.

"Maybe later," says Zada, uncertain to subject herself to too much this close to arrival from the future.

A receptionist who reminds Zada of a Barbie doll she once saw, eyes her up and down. "Cool threads," the girl says.

"What, are you also a fashion designer?"

"No...?" The girl says it as if it's a question.

Zada holds back from asking, "Are you doubting it?" Instead, she fingers shapely little packs in vivid wrappers inside a bowl on the counter. They look like lollies. "What are these?"

The girl perks up. "RATs."

"Say what?"

"Freebies. Take as many as you want. COVID-19 test kits. There's also an on-site nurse if you need one."

"Oh." Zada remembers John advised her that coronavirus became dormant sometime around 2023. Is there something for her to worry about? "I'm from out of town. We stopped doing these when the pandemic was scaled back to an epidemic."

"It's just a mandatory government requirement for big hotels. Everywhere has them but no-one ever takes the goodies, however pretty they may look. Even kids. They cry when you give them a shiny kit."

"Blows the mind, right?"

"You know how it is...politicians, votes...taxpayers' money to throw." The girl shrugs. "The nurses are whopper redundant, but they get paid big bucks."

"Maybe I should train to be one," says Zada. "You need money?"

"Not really."

The Tesseract secures her a private villa, homely like her flat in Carlton back in the future. She likes that it has a tropical rain shower in a dazzler green bathroom with surreal lights and fixtures that give the impression of a natural rainforest. There's also a stone washbasin with a spa, and she can step into it from an array of granite stones.

She's astonished to find a complimentary MacBook Pro laptop and a printer in the room, each coming alive on hand hover.

She's pleased to see a SocialBox icon on the desktop. She double-clicks on it to enter livestreams. She searches for Green, and there are pages and pages of forests, trees, paints, even a sea-sickness site called Tame the Green. She narrows her search to Jumping Time, and finds Green's series.

There he is, talking to her and the rest of the world about his time jumps. He has the blackest hair, and a piercing gaze. He is earnest, anxious, keen to connect with someone, others like him. As he talks, sometimes he looks sad, lonely. "I've missed a lot of things in my life," he says in his deep voice, in that first streaming that she knows verbatim. She searches for Us3r-Z, and is surprised to find that the profile doesn't exist.

She creates it on a whim. How about that? Now she is Us3r-Z. Green is live on SocialBox, in a familiar recording she knows verbatim.

"Hey mate, what's the date?" he says.

"Seventeenth July," Superscript25578 whips back.

"And the year?"

"The year? You got Old Timer's disease or something? It's 2028. All the way 'til the 31st December."

Her heart is pounding. Her fingers sticky on the keypad. There's a feature to send him a private message. She's afraid to trust it.

Finally, she types: "Maybe I can help. Let's meet."

Her message sits idle on the screen for what seems like forever. Finally, moving dots, someone is typing a message.

It's Green. "How can you help?"

Zada nearly cries for joy.

Chapter 12

She is goggle-eyed for lack of sleep. The espresso at Je Taime doesn't help much. Zada is in the worst state to be meeting Green, but she must. She's arrived early, way too early. It's just after 2 pm. And the scarved woman at the counter keeps popping by offering a treat of France, no matter how many times Zada says no.

"You want flan pâtissier? Is good. Half price."

"I'm good for now, thanks."

"Galette des rois, mmmh, frangipane. I give two, you pay one."

"Just another espresso, thanks."

Zada goes over in her head the conversation she'll have with Green. Her fascination with this man who has evolved into her life's purpose. She imagines his face, his relief, when she tells him she might be able to reset the Tesseract to stabilise his time jumps. And then what? She doesn't know—it's a start. Who knows? Perhaps it's fortuitous that her first meeting with Green is at a café named Je Taime?

She panics. What if she's arrived at the wrong place? But no. He said, "I'll be at Je Taime on Bourke Street, 3 pm." She looks at the Tesseract. 2.47 pm.

Suddenly there's commotion, and the woman at the counter is shouting. A whole crowd is surging in, shouting, "Green-o, Green-o!" They are kids mostly, pimpled teens in half-baked voices. Is that a filming crew? "Green-o, Green-o!" The chanting is as if they're at a religious convention, and the faithful are summoning the messiah.

The Frenchwoman is using a wooden spoon to beat away the raucous crowd from Je Taime. "Is *café*, not *le stade*! No hooligan!" But she's one, they are many.

Dammit! How the hell will Zada find Green amid all those bodies? She jumps, as someone lunges and knocks over her espresso.

"Bâtard!" The Frenchwoman shakes her wooden spoon, even as Zada wonders if she's truly French, but her thoughts are quickly lost as the crowd swells in her direction. She realises her clutch purse is lost, or one of those infantile pimple-heads has stolen it in the commotion. She's pushing bodies, feeling bodies. Please, oh, please. Frantic in her search.

And then the sirens.

Chapter 13

"Zis one, no." The Frenchwoman extracts Zada from the line-up of arrests. Zada can't believe how much richer the Frenchwoman's accent has turned.

A female cop uncuffs Zada. "Just an ID, please."

Zada stares at her, confused.

"I said your ID," the copper says.

"Wiz me!" the Frenchwoman says with ferocity, and tugs Zada from the line-up.

"We've been copping shit from anti-vaxxers," the copper says, almost apologetically. "One can't be too careful."

Zada should be relieved—how the hell would she have explained to the law her lack of records? "I'm from the future" certainly wouldn't have cut it. And the Tesseract!

It's nearly 5 pm now. If there's hell, this is hell. Zada is thinking up all sorts of worst-case scenarios as she helps the Frenchwoman rearrange the café. A robotic vacuum clears broken glass, mops up spills. Green never showed. If he did, then Zada lost him in the melee. Or maybe he's time jumped, unable to stop himself. And that's a worse scenario. Because Zada's lost the only thing that can take her to him.

Now Zada is seated, clasping with moroseness a tiny cup of espresso. Her mood has killed taste. The coffee is bland. No smoke or nut in it. Without the Tesseract, she's fucked.

"Zis." The Frenchwoman tosses a familiar purse onto the table. "For you."

"Oh!" Zada grabs at it. "Oh!" she says again. She looks inside—the Tesseract is intact.

She looks up, teary-eyed.

"You happy, is good for business," the Frenchwoman says.

Chapter 14

Back at the Diplomat, Zada lounges onto the bed, gazes at the ceiling. The white expanse allows her focus. An empty page. Since her jump—despite the wait in the café—she hasn't had opportunity to take a breath. Now it hits her. She is in the *past*. The facts are irrevocable. And however much she might have planned and prepared for this, the reality is somewhat different.

Something crawls in the pit of her stomach. She identifies the sensation as *loss*. Not of Green, although she remains frustrated that the opportunity to connect didn't arise, but of Tula, of John, of her parents. She forces herself immobile, fights not to pick up a phone and contact them. Not Tula or John, of course, she's not sure of their exact ages but they would be barely babes. And her parents wouldn't even have had *her* yet. Could she reach out? Could she prove who she was?

Talk about an identity crisis! She takes deeps breaths, rubs her forefingers against her thumbs on each hand. Gently, she stills her mind, fights the panic. Peeling her attention away from the white space that now seems like a void, she switches on the vidscreen, finds the news. There's footage of the disruption at Je Taime. She sits up, cross-legged. There's the Frenchwoman, a reporter's mike up her throat, being interviewed after Zada had already left. She's vocal, gesticulating wildly, as though signing in Auslan as well as speaking. Zada can't help but smile. Despite the transitory nature of the experience, watching the woman is like watching an old friend.

She skims the rest of the news. Other than the anti-vaxxers, there's bare mention of the pandemic. John was right. While she finds fascination with the world around her, Zada only briefly skips into other channels. She doesn't need to assimilate too much. She won't be here for long, now, after all.

She wonders about returning to the past again, just a few hours back, before the start of the demonstration. Could she wait outside Je Taime, keep an eye out for Green there? Would it be easier to pick him out? She runs a hand through her hair. If she did this, if she then pressed her face against the glass window and looked inside, would she see herself, sat there with an espresso, also waiting for Green to arrive?

She had discussed this with John. Once she arrives in the past, she then moves forwards in real time, so that the *actual* past also becomes her *lived* past. A sort of time reconciliation. While she never previously existed in 2028, she does now, and did a few hours ago. On paper, the easiest thing is to return and try for Green again, but how many reiterations can she go through until the demonstrators are outnumbered by Zadas? It isn't worth the risk.

She enters Jumping Time. Green is offline. She tries the private message feature, but it's greyed out. The hell? She slams shut the vidscreen, stares at it in frustration.

In the bathroom she takes a rainforest shower. She pushes her face forward into the jets, feeling the water take a circuit around the contours of her hair, her eyes, her mouth. She stays there longer than she intended. When she steps out, she realises that time is her own. She could forget the mission—stay a year or more here if she wanted to—enjoy the experience, and then go back further for Green. There's no-one to police her. Nothing can pull her back from the past. Suddenly she thinks of dizzying, giddying freedom.

Hot air vents dry her from all angles. She doesn't even need to turn. Zada remembers the disconnect Green described on SocialBox, his inability to stop hurtling towards infinity. She has that control. Her circumstances are different from his; but they now have that kinship. She understands his confusion, his vulnerability. She shakes doubts from her head and focuses on the mission. There'll be opportunities to experience the past once she hooks up with Green and is able to affect his future.

"See," she says aloud, to an A I Green who is yet to exist, "your psychological profiling was exact. I haven't gone off the rails…yet."

The private messaging function is still offline. She has no channel to connect with Green. Dammit. She must chase him deeper into the past, to another time.

Even so, she decides to remain in the present for a few more hours. For one, she needs to nap, and then she wants to visit where it all began.

She wants to see the Sarah Sands.

Chapter 15

The Barbie doll on reception was perceptive when it came to clubwear. Zada now sports an asymmetrical block-cut crop top in black and lime green which stops at her belly button, with a faux-leather black miniskirt over equally lime green leggings. She looks at herself in the mirror, wonders if it's her eyes, or maybe she looks a bit younger.

The girl had raised an eyebrow at Zada's destination.

"There's plenty of other clubs around here. Starfleet. Glamourama. Sub Club. We even have one right here in the hotel."

"So what's with the Sarah Sands?"

Barbie screws up her face. "Er...kinda, *traditional*." She says it as though the word is distasteful. Zada can't help but smile. All those clubs Barbie mentioned would be traditional to her.

"Oh, I have reasons," she says, with enough emphasis for the girl to understand there might be a guy involved.

The girl smiles wide. "I can book you a ride," she says. "Rolls Royce shuttles out front. And good luck."

Now Zada sits back in the Rolls Royce, watching a Melbourne she is half-familiar with zip by in the night. Darkness adds familiarity. It's as though this present is overlaid by her future, allowing her to see both simultaneously. She deconstructs the larger buildings in her mind's eye, assembles after-effects of neon light as though viewing constellations or making the connections in a dot-to-dot picture. The effect is disconcerting. She could almost be otherwhere. When she closes her eyes, she is here.

She pays for the ride with the Tesseract, exits the vehicle. The Sarah Sands Hotel is right before her. Her heart thrums in anticipation. She knows that here—for Green—on the dance floor—was where it all started. But also it's not impossible to imagine that he is here again now. Drawn like a salmon upriver to spawn. Over and over again.

The suited grunts at the door let her in. The floorspace is evenly split. Bar area to the right, club to the left. She wanders up to the counter, takes a stool. The music is retro to her, current here. She feels like hugging herself for how much she knows. Whopper high five.

The decor, the ambience, is upmarket. The grungy 'Kool Thing' would be out of place. She imagines the scene was much different in 1990: blackened walls, sticky dance floor, a pool table in the corner where the cues might quickly double as weapons. Zada knows her future was sanitised, understands that for Green this would be too. As Zada fixes her position at the bar and beckons over the bar staff—a fair girl in black trousers, white blouse, black waistcoat, ponytail blonde—she realises time travel is archaeology, peeling away past layers to find the one true experience. Yet for every layer removed, there's always another underneath.

She hasn't eaten. Her stomach is a whirl of knots. She orders the crispy halloumi with local honey, fig compote, pepperberry and mint. Her Tesseract completes the business.

After the waitress takes the order, she tarries alongside Zada a while until the girl finally decides to voice her curiosity. "Your method of payment. I haven't seen one of those. Is it new?" Colour rises in the girl's cheeks. "I mean, if you don't mind me asking."

Zada takes out the Tesseract again, glides it from one hand to the other. "It's a prototype," she says, "several devices in one."

"It looks futuristic!"

"Oh, it is!"

The girl takes time to serve someone at the other end of the bar. Zada's foot taps along to the beats. She scans the crowd for Green. She doesn't imagine he'll be dancing. She envisages him as a solo traveller, standing at the peripheries, looking for an opportunity to understand himself. She likes this, the idea of depth in him. Nothing shallow like some bozos she's dallied with.

Strobe lights jerk the patrons, their movements as staccato as zombies. Zada admires bodies. It's been 15 years since Tula was in her bed only that morning, the residue of potential strums along her senses hasn't dissipated. She finds herself eager for a hook-up.

The waitress returns with her food. Under the crisp exterior, the halloumi has a rubbery, semi-firm texture that squeaks between her teeth. The waitress is hovering again, clearly bored. Zada pushes the Tesseract between them on the counter. Presses a button.

Green's image flickers above the device, a hologrammatic display. "I'm looking for this guy," Zada says. "Have you seen him?"

The waitress seems more interested in the technology than in Green, but she shakes her head. "We get a lot of guys coming in here," she says. "As long as they bring no trouble, most blokes look the same to me."

Zada flips off the image, her eye catching hologram-Green's in the breadth of a second, as though a connection were possible. There is so much to assimilate she doesn't know where to begin.

There's movement on the seat beside her. "Fancy device."

Turning her head she sees white teeth set in a tanned face, blue eyes, a shock of dyed-silver hair. The guy wears an equally silver suit. He holds out a hand.

"Dalton."

She extends hers. "Zada."

"Exotic!" He shifts awkwardly, as if not used to stools, his eyes darting this way and that.

"You waiting for someone?"

"Apologies." Dalton turns full attention to her. "Haven't seen you before. You from out of town?"

Zada laughs. "You could say that." She realises again that the possibilities of time travel are freeing. She can be whoever, wherever she wants.

Dalton nods. He is short on conversation. She doesn't need it anyway. He's fit beneath the suit. An energy ripples from him that she could engage with. He reminds her of Gregg—*Gregg?* George. No, Gary—that morning of her SocialBox interview. She does the math. No, the man before her couldn't be Gary's father.

Her mind is turning, her mouth speaking. Her words fall naturally, fill a backstory for Dalton that even she won't remember. The waitress glances over on occasion, now at the other end of the bar. Zada sees jealousy there, but isn't sure which of them it is directed at. A ménage à trois pops into her head. Her—the girl—Dalton. How easy it would be to arrange. Dalton is there already, his hand now hovering above her knee, like a helicopter trying to land in a storm. Zada is still eating: she images spearing the halloumi and making an offering, watching Dalton eat it from the fork before she then shares another bite. All the signals, the biological echoes are here, all she has to do is make a move.

Mere moments from this she checks herself. She stands, places a hand on Dalton's shoulder. "Wait here." She crosses the floor to the bathroom. She feels everyone's eyes on her. Not only those present, but all those who have occupied the Sarah Sands from the moment of its inception until beyond her own future.

She splashes water onto her face. In the adjacent men's toilet, 38 years previously, Green would have done the same: taking stock after his first time jump. Zada looks into her eyes. She realises she's going to decline what Dalton hasn't even broached yet. She surprises herself with this decision, but suddenly casual flings with those who in her own time are so much older than her feels too arbitrary. Tenuous it might be, but there is a connection with Green. They are two of a kind.

She returns to the bar, walks past Dalton. But it doesn't matter. Dalton has already propositioned another. Zada is okay with that. She wanders across to the dance floor, finds the energy enervating. She throws her hands in the air, dances to the beats of her parents, becomes embroiled in the moment, her feet side-stepping, turning, performing. Wherever she is, she is in the present. She soaks it up. Closes her eyes. Is lost in music.

Chapter 16

Zada pays for the taxi she's taken from downtown Melbourne to Collingwood. She nearly took a tram, hoping the Tesseract also worked as a myki travel pass. She should have. The taxi driver was one of the talkative types, barrelling along about cricket so much that Zada didn't have the heart to tell him that, in her future, people don't play cricket any more.

She time jumped the morning after her Sarah Sands dance night, glad to have awoken solo in bed, finding herself strangely thinking of Green. She wonders why—she doesn't even know the man that well! Other than what A I Green chose to share with her, and how intimately she got to know Green, almost verbatim, from his Jumping Time series, and then the brief private messaging they'd shared...But they do have the connection of being two different people soaring out of time.

The Tesseract is set back 10 years to 2018. She knows Green missed his father's wedding, but doesn't know if he paid many visits after. Back in the future John did some research and, via the 2026 census, identified the property on Turner Street where she's hoping Green's father still resides.

Number 4 is a big and grey period structure with flowered awnings. She strides up to the front door, the butterflies in her stomach belying outward confidence. This is the first time she's meeting someone who actually knows Green. Zada finds herself uncommonly conflicted.

She raps on the door. Loud music belts out of the upstairs windows. It's too raucous for her, but she takes on that sentiment. Fancy that, she's getting physically younger but her mind is older, hopefully wiser.

A gangly teen opens the door. "'Sup?" he eyes her, not seeing her. He's bare-chested, skinny jeans with torn knees, a tiny hint of stubble on his chin.

Zada sees a hint of Green in him. Perhaps the piercing eyes. But that's where the resemblance is lost. He's ginger-haired, too tall.

"Well?" he says, surly.

"Shano!" A woman calls from somewhere inside. "It's not the Jehovah Witness peeps again, is it?"

"N-nope," he says. Swings the door wide.

A woman, perhaps in her fifties, pushes past him.

"Why, hello. What's this?" the woman says.

Zada's lack of words shames her. She never imagined she'd actually meet Green's family. The boy—Shano, Shane?—must be his half-brother.

"Are...Are you Sharee?" Zada finally says awkwardly—already knowing *she is* Sharee.

"Why, dear, yes." There's a natural husk in Sharee's voice. "Don't mind Shane, his lack of manners. I taught him well, I promise. Please!" She steps aside.

Shano scowls and vanishes into what might be a downstairs bedroom, or man cave, and its blare of all that music.

"And will you turn that thing down, jeez!" yells Sharee in his direction.

The sound in the music dips.

Sharee has raised the boy well, notes Zada.

"He used to be nuts about footy," the older woman says. "Now the rage is all music."

A soft Turkish carpet spreads all the way around a living room. Zada removes her shoes.

"Oh, please, don't," says Sharee.

But Zada arranges the shoes outside the carpet, near the hallway.

"Masterpiece," says Zada. She feels the carpet and its reds, blues and golds with her bare toes. "Pure silk?"

"Something classic. Persian. Willie has a penchant for them."

Will, Green's dad.

"Is he home?" asks Zada hesitantly.

Sharee stares at her hands for a moment, and Zada panics. She sinks into a sofa so soft, she's afraid she might not be able to rise from it. What if Green's father is dead? Then Sharee breaks into a disarming smile. "Coaching footy. Kids. He's taken a shining to the little ones, sometimes I think it's his penance for…"

"Green?" suggests Zada.

Sharee makes her comfortable. Something about the older woman reminds Zada of Asante, and she doesn't think it's age or the bohemian V-neck sweeping to Sharee's ankles.

"Dear me." Sharee doesn't answer the question. "That boy has infected me with his poor manners. Tea?"

"Yes please. No sugar."

"You'll take anything?"

"Sure."

"How about some fresh mint?"

"Sounds divine."

Zada imagines the older woman's glow when she was pregnant with Shane. She imagines her as a mother trying to contain a fat-legged toddler wriggling in her arms, keen to set down and wander—the boy must have been a bit of a handful. Zada pictures him as a four-year-old, all buzzed up, slushed out, terrorising a carnival—his mother's hand only a reach away. Something Green never had.

Sharee is back in a jiffy, a teapot straight from *Aladdin and the Magic Lamp* on an antique serving tray fashioned with dainty handles.

"Please tell me you're not one of those skinny things that pass up on a good honey cake," she says.

"Me? Never," says Zada.

She marvels at Sharee's kindness, her patience with a total stranger who's arrived at her doorstep only armed with names: Sharee, Green, Will.

"You haven't asked me—"

"Why you're here?" says Sharee. "Where's the fun in that?"

They laugh.

Zada looks at her squarely. "What if I told you I'm from the future?"

"Are you?"

"Yes."

"Okay," says Sharee.

"Just like that?" asks Zada astounded. "You believe me?"

"You say you're from the future, then you're from the future—unless you've got rocks in your head, which I don't think so." Sharee clasps her hands. "Yes, forgive my intrusion, but I think now I will ask. Why are you here?"

"Green. When did you last see him?"

Sharee throws her arms. "He and Willie never had a good start in life. I just wish..." She looks at Zada. "He doesn't visit. His brother..." She shakes her head. "Shano...I think he... Green..." Finally, she just says it. "You know, Green could have been more to that kid."

"What if he can't visit, Sharee?"

"Is he...he's not..." Sharee can't bring herself to say it.

"No, he's not dead." Zada pushes herself from the sofa's gulp, and kneels before the older woman and her sadness. "Green is conflicted about many things. He's time jumping into the future, and I'm here to help him."

There's a long silence as Sharee takes this all in, unquestioning. "I don't get it," she says at last. "He did miss our wedding by six months..."

"I need you to believe what I'm going to tell you next," says Zada gently.

"Oh, I believe you," says Sharee. "And I remember you, although I can't quite believe I'm saying this. You were at our wedding reception in 1991, and you haven't aged a single bit. If anything, you look younger. Gracious me."

Chapter 17

The visit with Sharee went better than Zada could have hoped. She's never met anyone so...accepting of her?

In the end, Zada declined to wait for Will, and gently but firmly declined Sharee's generous offer for Zada to stay with them a few days. Because, suddenly, in the course of the visit, Zada felt overwhelmed.

"It's no big deal," Sharee said, understanding almost immediately. Empathy, telepathy, as if she was a mind reader, attuned to Zada. "Come, dear, I'll see you to the door."

Zada rose, grateful.

"Shano, Zada's leaving," Sharee called.

"Yo," the teen said, and turned up the music.

Yet, even as she left, Zada hoped she wouldn't regret it.

Now she wishes she didn't miss her own parents Asante and Bakari this much. Sharee has infused in her a longing for family—she's never seen so much trust and affection before. And from a total stranger. Well, not now.

Despite all that, the connection with Sharee, it's useless for Zada's quest. Sharee had no clue where Green might be, and suggested that maybe Bateman might know.

"Will says they were besties, until...Who knows what happens between two grown men?" Sharee said.

Chapter 18

Zada takes a cab to Ringwood. Green had talked about a Lilydale line from Flinders, but she's all shook from the visit with Sharee, and she doesn't really want to waste time dillydallying with trains and timetables.

The lawn at the townhouse on Nelson Street is jungle. A cat stirs litter. It slinks behind the end of a long queue of yellow bins as Zada approaches. It's a witch's cat, all black, turquoise eyes. It peers, as if asking *why?* She too wants to know why. How the cat brings with it memories of petting a rooster named Rose way back in the Dandenong Ranges. Zada, to this day, has never understood why anyone would name something that might end up in a pot sooner rather than later if she had a say. She thinks of her mother, a silent shape gazing at her dreams as she sleeps. Zada wants to know why her mother is here. She wants to know why she, Zada, is not a child any more—too late now to reach for her mother. Because Zada has grown too quickly. Such irony. In essence, she's getting a touch younger deeper into the future.

She looks away from the glow of the cat's eyes, and rings the bell. Silence. How long to wait? She rings it again, again, again.

Finally, a man opens the door. He's unkempt, sunken into himself. "Bateman? My name is Zada. I'm here to talk about Green."

He wordlessly turns and allows her to follow him up a floor into a room crawling with wall plants. The timbered floor is full of cracks and scratches. There are piles of clothing, newspapers, dirty plates everywhere. Zada has nowhere to sit, and the man doesn't offer any options.

"What about Green?" he says haggardly.

She tries to tell him, but Bateman takes way more to convince than Sharee. Zada goes for honesty, because that's her way. But he won't listen, even after the Tesseract comes into play, and Zada has to "prove" that she's from the future.

"What were you planning to do today?" she asks Bateman.

"Footy. Bombers and Sainters killing themselves at the G."

She resets the Tesseract, then rings the bell. Silence. What if the timing is botched—the joke would be on her, wouldn't it? She rings and rings again, again, again. Bateman opens the door. Unkempt, sunken into himself.

"Bateman?" she says. "My name is Zada. I'm here to talk about Green."

When he says, "What about Green?" she says, "Footy. Bombers and Sainters killing themselves at the G. You're going, aren't you?"

"Bloody hell! How would you know a thing like that?"

"I'm from the future. And you told me a few minutes ago that you were going to the footy."

"Fuck off."

"You punched Green when he came to see you after Ali… passed. And he tripped on a garden gnome."

"The hell?"

"He pounded on the door, but you wouldn't let him in."

"What the actual fuck?"

"You and he sat back to back against the door, still you wouldn't open, and he left."

"Is this a fucking joke?"

"He tried to tell you, many times, Bateman."

"Tell me about fucking what?"

"About slipping time. Green was time jumping, Bateman, and he tried to tell you, but you refused to believe him. You let him down when he needed you the most."

"I…I *let him down*? *I* let him…? Fuck it! He was my mate, and he let me down! I lost my whole fucking family. And he let me down!"

Bateman breaks down. Big manly sobs that are terrible to hear. Zada pats his back awkwardly, puts his head against her bosom, as she might for the brother she never had. But damn! It's pretty messy.

They are standing, and he is bawling and hiccupping, clinging to her, as she sways him, until he's silent. Still, she holds him. He's a big bloke, but somehow now he's on the floor, bum down, knees jutting up, helpless as a little boy, and she's folded alongside him.

"How about you spruce up and we go to the footy together, where I'll tell you all I know about Green?" she says gently.

Chapter 19

The crowd is psyched, garbed in footy colours at the Melbourne Cricket Ground—the G, as Bateman calls it.

It's a pre-season game between Essendon and St Kilda—the Bombers and the Sainters, as Bateman calls them, and Zada is not expecting to be rubbing shoulders with celebs.

The Sainters' skipper wins the toss and picks a side to kick their goals. Each team is weighing up a decent share of young bucks, fresh recruits off the draft—barely out of school yet taller than Apollo. They're keen to show themselves, and are impacting the scoreboard, changing the momentum as the crowd roars. One Bombers rookie is pulsing the stadium.

"Flashed it!"

"Two in a row!"

"He's a beautiful kick!"

Other players are playing delicate, avoiding injuries this early, pre-season, as they settle into the game. The sun is setting, long shadows on the grass.

At half-time, the Bombers are leading. Zada goes to the hawker stand, grabs pies and VBs. The siren goes again. The lads are running, bounding in tight jumpers and little shorts. The rookie comes all the way down the end of the oval to hold possession. He loses the ball but works up the wings, scrambling, body work, pushing hard and breaking defence. He kicks with good footy skills, and each boot puts plenty on the ball. He glides a sider that goes for home, then—seemingly almost immediately—another thumper that puts scores on the board.

"Makes them pay!" screeches a commentator.

"This is gonna hurt!"

The Sainters charge him, open the kid up early, blood spatter on his jumper. He gets stitched up and is back knocking the ball around. Zada watches, entranced. She's always been outdoorsy, and this rookie is the deal. He's all strapped up, coping harassment-type pressure from players on the other team. But this kid just strolls in and kicks another goal.

The commentators go wild:

"Easy game. Kicks three in a row!"

"Pandemonium! How's the wow on that boot?"

"The beauty of it!"

The kid runs—knees jumping, fists pounding his chest—to the crowd at the wings. His body tells them all about it, what they already know. That he's a genius!

The G erupts. As the noise settles, Bateman turns to Zada, who's holding a pie in one hand, a tinny in the other.

His eyes are glowing.

"What's your team?" Zada asks. "You've been cheering everybody."

"Like Christ at the footy," he says. "Townsville, Noosa—I got stuck with the Lions. I go for Brissie."

"The Brisbane Lions?"

"The best," he says, and studies her for a long time, as if forgetting the game. Then, quietly, "You really from the future?"

"Depends on your belief. Do you believe?"

He shrugs. "What's belief?"

"Belief is an acceptance of truth or existence without proof," says Zada, surprising herself by answering as A I Green would.

"Deep. Who says that?" Bateman says.

"A...friend," says Zada. "A pal." She feels an intense affection for A I Green. And a missing. She misses home.

"Brissie has an away game at the G next Saturday arvo. A nighter. You wanna come?"

"Sure. I'll be staying at the Sarah Sands Hotel. Pick me up there."

"It's a date," he says solemnly.

"With no benefits."

"There's a bit on it." He grins at her raised brow. "Relax. We're just chilling."

Chapter 20

Zada gets a modern studio at the Sarah Sands Hotel in New Brunswick. It's an en suite, nothing close to the Diplomat, even though it offers laundry, business services, free wi-fi in its deluxe rooms. The queen bed feels tiny, as does the kitchenette with a mini fridge, a microwave and an electric kettle. Compared to what she's accustomed to, even what she had at the Diplomat, these are Zinjanthropan standards.

She looks forward to seeing Bateman again. Watching with him beautiful low passes on the field. Kids maximising what they can, too easy. Kids going *snap!* with a boot. Balls ricocheting in benders through the middle. Commentators yelling out loud:

"What. About. That?"

"He was. Never gonna. Miss that!"

"He's. Got it!"

Knowing Bateman feels like knowing Green. Even in his worst state, unkempt, dishevelled, Bateman represents a different kind of man, unlike those in her future. Unlike Gary and his soft hands, soft mouth, chic sunnies. In her mind, Bateman is at one with those bucks at the oval, kicking the ball long and strong. Men tough as they come, charging at the footy, causing tumblers in a traffic of bodies. Men giving the ball straight, hooked or banana, opening paths from the halfway flank, playing on even when they are outnumbered. Men defending well, meeting head and shoulder in solid contests that break the ball even from impossible positions. Sidestep, good kick, quickly on the boot. Ball reeling, steering all the way home. This is how she imagines Green.

It takes her forever to sleep, the beef pies and beer uneasy in her stomach. She wakes in the dead of the night with a croak. Her head is on fire. Her throat is burning, burning, and the pies and VB are running right through her. She's munting all night, wrenching her guts out. She trips many times in a dash to the bathroom, and her body feels weak.

In her fevered head, she panics. What if she's patient zero, bringing a pandemic to this world?

She fumbles with the RAT she took with her from the Diplomat, and wonders if the Sarah Sands might have a nurse on call. She puts the RAT on her tongue and absorbs its sweetness, then looks at it. Nothing. It's not COVID.

By midday of the following day, her skin has broken in rashes. Her stomach is not holding anything from the mini fridge, not even the apple juice or sparkling water. She tries dried crackers and retches them out until her guts almost fall out of her mouth. Her whole body is still burning, burning, aches and pains. She crawls to bed, and passes out.

Somewhere in the distance, a phone ringing, ringing. She groans, tries to put a pillow over her head, because each ring is a monstrous bell, an axe splitting her head.

Somewhere in her dreams, men running, running in little shorts. Handsome men, pretty crude. Brutes on the oval, guts on the field. A ball ploughs through the posts. There's Green, charging at the footy in the last millisecond, doing magic with his boot.

She cries herself to sleep.

Now it's dark, now it's day. How many days?

She wonders, if she dies now, here in the past, would her future change? Perhaps she'd simply evaporate, disintegrate, her body ceasing to exist. What would her parents' future look like? This past has no return.

The phone again, ringing, ringing. She is a mouse, a newspaper, floating to nowhere. She's a bird, stiff, going in, into the belly of a monstrous snake. If she could write to her own body, it would be a script in the language of song. 'Kool Thing'. She is burning, burning.

Ring. Ring.

At the edge of her vision, her door opens. And then hands. Touching, moving her. A towel on her face. The silhouette of a man. He is talking to her, not talking. Putting liquid into her mouth through a straw, begging her to suck, please suck, just a little. She draws weakly, and the liquid is heaven. But she has no strength. He's dry-washing her, talking tenderly as she slips in and out of consciousness.

A flock of white pigeons descends on the oval, a snow of birds on a green, green pitch. Zada sleeps through all that green and all that snow.

The pigeons become a bunch of male and female players, and they can take tackles. Men and women serious about the ball pinging around the snow-white oval, and they manoeuvre and convince the footy their way. Men and women who understand risk versus reward, and plough at you to kill the other team's ball. They run and jump at it. Long penetrators.

Commentators shouting.

"They. Are. Raining. Goals!"

"Forty-five-degree angle. He'll take it!"

She dreams about Tula. She dreams about Green.

Chapter 21

She comes to, fully.

"You're awake."

She looks at him. The lights in the room hurt her eyes. She knows him. It's Bateman. She tries to speak, but can only groan.

"Gave us quite the fright," he says.

"How...did...you?" she finally whispers.

"You told me the Sarah Sands," he says. "Glad I didn't wait until Saturday to check on you."

He looks rejuvenated, as if her sickness and his caring for her has given him purpose.

"It...wasn't...COVID," she says.

"What's a coveed?"

"Oh." She remembers the pandemic hasn't happened yet. "Maybe food poisoning."

"Or your future is rejecting our past."

"So you believe." She smiles wanly. "John said..."

"Who's John?"

"Never mind." She tries to sit. Bateman helps her. He arranges the pillows at her back. "Batey." She grips his hand.

"Don't talk. You need the strength."

"Thank you."

"It's nothing." He squeezes her hand. "But you owe me a game under the lights at the G."

Chapter 22

They don't drive to the G.

"I want to enjoy a pint," says Bateman.

"A pint, or three?" teases Zada.

Batey is a big bloke, yet a gentle giant. Zada suspects he's the kind who's considerate inside or outside the car. He wouldn't swear at other drivers in it. And, outside a car, he wouldn't traumatise a distracted elderly driver by getting himself knocked down at a zebra crossing. He'd probably stand, patient by the sidewalk, perhaps even smile, knowing too well that he had the right of way.

Bateman looks elated after the match. Brissie beat the Bombers 84 points to 62. Zada can't help but love this game. Muscled men sleek as cheetahs, players who understand space.

The commentators nearly gobble their mikes over a fast forward with a boot.

"Left foot has a journey!"

"He's in for a big season!"

Bateman is glowing. Zada can tell her presence adds to the fervour of his demeanour. He's a changed man from when she first met him. Nothing like the rut she found inside a house choked up with plants. She wonders what he would have been like around his wife and kids. How cruel to have that taken away. No wonder Bateman blames Green. He has to blame someone. She wonders how he'll fare during the upcoming pandemic. It's much easier to fight people than it is to fight disease. You can't see cancer—COVID—whatever—with the naked eye. How do you rail against that?

Chapter 23

They are back at the Sarah Sands, at the bar.

"He caught me at a bad moment," Bateman says, out of the blue. He's staring at his VB.

Zada doesn't answer. She knows he's talking about Green. She's on a Native Lilly Pilly, Lemon Myrtle & Wild Lavender Drinking Shrub. She's gone for non-alcoholic. She doesn't intend on fuzzing her consciousness again. She wants a clear head around Bateman. There's a draw to him, an appeal that she's resisting. She notices his teeth—so white, silver flakes on them catching the light. He's a brother and a friend. He's a "more" kind of thing she doesn't want to put a name on, because yoga sex is *not happening* with this man. No. No. Never.

"Green hadn't been around for years," he's saying. "I'd gone through all that shit without him. Didn't know if he was dead or alive. Then he comes at me with that time jump stuff and I just flew at him. You would, wouldn't you?"

Her smile is non-committal. She doesn't know what she'd do if she were Bateman.

"And I was so...out of it too," says Batey. "I did try to contact him afterwards, but again it was like he'd disappeared into thin air. I just took it that I'd blown him off, and I was too angry to make proper enquiries. Even though deep down I missed the bugger." He looks at her, the scar on his face dancing. "So, where's the champ now?"

Zada shakes her head. "Truth is, I was hoping you could tell me."

"You can't track him with that future gumbo?"

"Green is moving uncontrollably into the future. He's recorded some pivotal instances in that journey which allows me to get a handle on him, but nothing's precise. I'm trying to stop him before he goes too far ahead. Like, maybe into infinity."

Bateman rubs a hand over his chin. Zada sees it clearly, the sorrow and regret in his eyes. Green wasn't only not there for Bateman, but Bateman now realises he hasn't been there for Green.

"Shit. So he could literally be in a future where none of us exists? That's...that's just lonesome."

Zada imagines he's thinking of his daughter Ali, long gone, of his wife and maybe other kids, of himself. Of the loneliness that visits everyone at some point. Of the loneliness at the end — of what?

She thinks of her own connections — Asante, Bakari, Tula, A I Green, perhaps even Green himself — and wonders whether life might be better without any of them. A solo emotionless journey. Do humans evolve consciousness just to be hurt?

"Maybe we're better off as plants," she says to no-one.

Bateman just nods, he doesn't ask her to elaborate. It's as if he understands, deeply understands.

Perhaps just as Green's freedom in moving forward in time conflicts with his knowledge that he'll outstrip everyone he knows, that one day they'll all be dead and him still living, Zada sees that any freedom she's felt about going into the past conflicts with everyone who was in her timelines, but here they're not even born. In some way, she and Green have a bond. They're equal in that loneliness.

She realises Bateman's hand is on her shoulder. It's a comfort, but their only shared connection is Green, and she realises they're both acting as substitutes for him.

"You okay?" Bateman asks. "Not going to throw up on me again?"

"Did I actually *do* that?"

"You might as well have done." Bateman laughs. "What happens in a room stays in a room. A good man doesn't tell."

"Oh, we're good now, are we?"

"Always. Green knew this." He goes pensive, sadder even. "I miss the bloke," he says again.

Zada sips from her drink. Ziggy's Wildfood products are also in her future, and that combination of unique and incredibly aromatic flavours really sends her home.

"Tell me more about Green," she says.

"It'll help you trace him?"

"I won't lie, no. Just so it will help me understand."

Chapter 24

They're still at the Sarah Sands, the bar happy to take their money. Bateman wants to be the man, pay for it all, but Zada insists on a tab to her room.

If Bateman's not sure what Zada's driving at in her questioning of him, he doesn't show it.

He necks from the bottle of VB. Wipes his mouth. "Green and I went travelling together. There's a bond there that can't be broken. Two guys in a camper. No commitments. The naivety of youth. We headed up to Queensland. Noosa. Townsville. The usual. Spent a lot of time around the Whitsundays. Camped out on the beach with fruit bats chittering above us in the trees, their crap bouncing off the tent." He laughs deeply, now. "One of those ovals dropped into Green's cup of tea. I let him take a sip before I said anything."

He roars. They're laughing together. His teeth white as white.

"Jeez, those pure white sands at Whitehaven Beach," says Bateman. "And the girls—a few of those too. But Green had to work harder than I did. He's more thoughtful, lives less in the moment, you know." Bateman pauses. "Although I imagine living in the moment is all he has now."

"What else did you do together?"

"We went snorkelling off the Whitsundays. Back then it felt more laid back than at Cairns. I imagine that's all changed now. I remember floating in that azure blue, dodged by wrasse, hearing the *peck peck* of parrot fish nibbling the coral, when a massive turtle swam just beneath me. Man, those days were perfect. We hung around Brisbane for a while. There was a good club there. I don't remember the name, but Green would. He was always into his music, more alternative than me. I took that to be his Pommy background. If I was into Midnight Oil, he'd be moping around to The Cure, you know. That's what he took seriously, more than anything. Music."

"Why so, I wonder?"

"Looking back, it was a retreat. A sanctuary from those arguments his parents got into. He never talked about it, but there was always a frisson when I went round there, to that Essendon home. When they moved on, I suggested he sell it, but he could never do so. The ties that bind, eh?"

Zada nods. She's warming to Green with his insular lifestyle, the parental disconnect.

"He used to come here a lot," Bateman says, gesturing around them. "But I guess you know that."

Zada nods. "He recorded it. His first time jump was right there, on the dance floor."

Bateman appears to be thinking, doing the math in his head. "Would have been around 1990, right? I was with Tammy by then. I remember Green-o was a day late for work. Was convinced it was a Friday. I was hard on him. Man, if only I could have known..."

Now it's Zada's turn to place her fingers on Bateman's arm. "If you'd known, you still couldn't have done anything."

"No. But I would have understood. All those years later, I wouldn't have *decked* him. The poor sap."

"They say hindsight is a wonderful thing."

Bateman nods. "Nostalgia too. Thinking back to those Queensland days, when we were young and full of ourselves, no idea of all the shit to come." He picks up her fingers. Entwines them in his. "It's been a long time since I've spoken this much to anyone."

Zada sees where this might go. She doesn't want to hurt Bateman. In her time, this was a yoga sex beckoning moment. But she feels sleeping with Bateman would somehow hurt herself. Would hurt Green. She can't put a finger directly on where that stems from. But she knows it's correct. And it would hurt Bateman too. She gently withdraws her fingers.

Thankfully Bateman seems to understand without her having to spell it out. His rubs his chin again. "I guess you have nostalgia too. Nostalgia for the future."

"The future is my past," Zada says. She smiles. "And I guess the past is also my future."

Bateman finishes his VB in one long swallow. Puts the bottle down on the bar. "Headfuck!"

A moment of silence spins between them. Zada wonders if Bateman will ask questions. Who wouldn't, presented with someone from the future? Maybe he'll enquire about the state of the planet, if there's anything she can warn him about. Should she tell him about the pandemic? Maybe he's thinking about next week's Lotto numbers. Maybe he's wondering if she knows about his death. Truth is, she's unaware of Bateman being alive in 2050. She also gulps down the last of her drink.

"I guess you're leaving soon," Bateman says. "You told me you can't travel forward, right? So what happens if you altogether miss Green?"

It's the elephant in her room. If she doesn't meet Green, she can't work out how he's jumping. If she can't work that out, then she's stuck in the past.

"I don't want to think about it. Hey, that Friday you mentioned when Green thought it was Saturday. Do you have a date for that?"

Bateman's laugh is hollow. He knows what she's thinking. "So you can pinpoint his first jump, here in this hotel? No, I can't recall that. Can you remember that many years back?"

He glances at Zada. "There might be records at Boeing, but no, scrap that. I covered for Green."

"You're a good man, Bateman."

Bateman shrugs. "We are what we are."

Chapter 25

Zada can't help it—she times the Tesseract and travels further back in time to 1995. She's eager to finish this. These conversations with Bateman are forging interactions that imprint on her how lonely she is.

She takes the number 234 from Flinders Street Station. In 20 minutes, it turns into Lorimer Street in Port Melbourne.

She hadn't realised the Boeing factory would be Fort Knox— she can't get past the gate.

"Just get Bateman for me, please," she says. "Tell him it's about Green."

He comes to the gate. He's younger, more bouncy than before when she met him.

"Yes?"

He doesn't remember her, of course he wouldn't remember a future he hasn't experienced. Yet it deflates her. A connection unforged.

"I'm...I'm here about Green," she says.

"Yes?" he says again, in a non-committal, almost impatient way. He has a way of blocking himself, emotionally closed. She can't tell if he's interested or not. She glances at the guard, also listening.

"You want a coffee? Maybe we can talk...in private."

"Yeah," he says in that non-committal way, as if he doesn't care either way. "Across the road."

The café is not across the road, not as close as he suggested. It's about 150 metres ahead, waterside, in a business complex that houses lawyers and whatnots. A scatter of empty tables: two-seaters and fours on the ground floor. It's a tiny joint that could do with more patrons—anyone coming out the lift would see it. The café's counter is opposite a concierge. There's an egg benedict with ham hollandaise on special. Smoothies called

Acai Kick, Green Fever, Mango Dream, Pineapple Sunset. A Mediterranean toastie with avo halloumi. A breakfast called the Spartan. Overhead, a monitor with ticking headlines.

"Please let me." Zada offers to pay in the big silence of the café. "After all, I brought you here."

"Sure."

She looks at him expectantly. "You're not one of those soya decaf mocha types, no?"

"Oh, yeah, nah." He laughs, and it breaks the ice. "Catch me dead drinking that shit. A quad shot cappuccino, please."

She gets an espresso for herself, pays with the Tesseract.

"I'd fancy one of those." Bateman points at it.

Zada simply smiles.

They sit outside, black tables with orange chairs, a black umbrella, although it's mid-morn and the sun is not out.

"You a friend of Green's?" he asks.

She nods.

"Good. He can use more friends."

"You're mates, aren't you?"

"It's not like I get up thinking today I gotta see Green. Nah." Bateman shakes his head. "Look, I don't wanna talk shit—he's not here to defend himself."

She touches his arm. "We're talking among friends."

"Baffles me, the bloke. He was always a lost little boy, looking for his dad. I try to be a mate, a brother. But I can't play dad for a grown-ass man." He looks at her, almost angrily. "You find him, tell him to show up for work."

"Hasn't he been?"

"Bloke shows, bloke doesn't. Trying hard not to fire his ass, but the prick's not making it easy."

He looks at her, instantly apologetic. "My bad, why am I saying all this? I feel like I know you."

She takes his hands in hers across the table. "Maybe you do, Batey."

Chapter 26

Several times she visits the house in Essendon. No-one's home, but the first time she sees signs of habitation. Someone lives here. Green lives here! She stalks the property for a week. Turns up at different hours of the day and night. Peeks through the letterbox, sees mail littered on the welcome mat. She peers through grimy windows, makes out the L-shaped kitchen, the open plan living room. A mattress is on the floor of what must be Green's bedroom.

It's not quite squalor, but there's not much care to the place. She imagines each window as a portal to the past. Zada casts shapes of Green's parents into the mix, plays out scenes of his childhood, superimposed speculation over reality. Watches in her mind's eye as he shelters in this room, hiding from the arguments—his head under the bedclothes, the desperation in his young eyes for his parents to stop. She pictures Green's mother leaving the property, slamming closure on his young life, the fly screen door unhinging. She thinks of Will unable to care for his son, Will eventually leaving too. She sees Green on that mattress, curled into himself, desolate and alone.

In her final trip here, she finds the house boarded up, graffiti covering the plywood. A sold sign rammed into uncut grass.

She sits, despondent, at Essendon Station, looks up each time passengers step out of a train and onto the platform. None of them is Green. What now? She finds resonance in *The Great Gatsby*. Those final lines: *So we beat on, boats against the current, borne back ceaselessly into the past.*

Her imagination fills in the blanks. She hallucinates an evening where Green's mattress is occupied, a shock of black hair under the covers. But before she can tap on the window he fizzles as if strobe lighting has lit him, and he winks out of existence.

Chapter 27

Zada never realised she was such a critic. John had primed her for fashions in the early 90s, but she's wondering whether it was the decade that taste forgot. Graphic print Hawaiian shirts are wall to wall in high street stores, while the women are sporting strappy tops, tattoo-style chokers, scrunchies and cowrie shell jewellery. Barrettes, hair slides and stylised bobby pins aren't just for kids.

Zada decks herself out in a plaid midi-length slip skirt, dressed down with a band T-shirt—just who are ACDC anyway?—and throws a denim jacket over the top. She draws the line at risking the Tesseract in a bum bag, preferring to keep it in her regular purse which looks properly futuristic right now.

Despite the cringeworthy styles she wouldn't get for free in a thrift store in her future, she senses most people here are quite happy and wealthy. It's just that their clothing hasn't caught up with them yet.

Everywhere she walks, there seem to be couples of all ages, hand in hand, content with their lives. Sure, couples are mostly publicly heterosexual—she hasn't seen much alternative activity outside the Saturday night dance club known as Tasty, situated in a five-storey building at Flinders Lane, where the clientele are mainly gay and transgender, unpretentious, and Zada feels at home there, fluid on the dance floor.

But, predominantly, 1991 seems to be a time of plenty, long before bank crashes and disease took hold. In her eyes, there's an innocence to these scenes that play out before her: the kids yet to grow up, and the adults to follow suit. It creates an ache in the pit of her stomach for simpler times. Not just those here, but those in her own youth before she became disconnected from Asante and Bakari, and started longing for the way out that's led to this life. And it creates an ache for a connection, for contact.

And she misses Green—she actually misses him—this man she so badly wants to meet. She also misses Bateman. He's got Tammy and the kids around him now. The happiness before the heartbreak.

She wants to visit, but it wouldn't be right. And she can't clasp at the future, which is a past. A no-return past. First, he wouldn't know her. She'd have to explain herself again and he's not yet of an age where he'd be ready to hear it. He hasn't yet gone through the kind of trauma that makes one believe. Second, while Bateman didn't give the impression that Tammy was the jealous sort, the arrival of a woman with an unbelievable backstory would take more than an honest explanation. Besides, Bateman has already told her everything about Green that she needs. He'll know even less now, the further into *his* past that she digs. Batey's absence is another loss for her. One she must recover from.

She spends most nights alone, amusing herself with television shows that never made it to repeats. Sometimes she considers news items—like the Gulf War—which must have seemed so worrying at the time, but is now already in her ancient history. The passing of time feels such a fluid construct to her. She's like a grayling caught in a coastal tide.

Other nights she thumbs through paperbacks, plays with her body to a discontent beat. She finds herself flicking back again and again through the information she holds on Green. She accesses his image, rotates him front and back, considers his features under that black-as-black hair. She finds that she likes him without knowing him. There's a troublesome innocence in his countenance which suggests he's a decent guy.

There's nothing in his history to suggest he's abused his power. He's not settled any scores or time jumped out of responsibility. It's not like she's been sent back in time to kill him. She laughs at this.

She finds herself looking deeper into his eyes—not that he can look back, the technology isn't *that* great, no holograms here—wondering what exactly he's feeling. It's not as though he has the control that she does. Those initial jumps must have been disorientating, frightening. There would have been no understanding of what was happening, or why. As the focal point for her mission, the urge to save him has gone beyond a business-like fascination.

She wants to *know* him, intimately. To understand what makes him tick. Share his likes and dislikes. Share the whole time travel story with him. She wants to share *her* story with him.

This decision to be with him, physically, to reassure, to *reset*, consumes her thoughts, over and above the remit of her job.

Because it's no longer a job. It's personal.

Chapter 28

It's February. The date of Will and Sharee's wedding. Zada's aware that Green never attended. She set the Tesseract for six months after the event, but the variable accuracy brought her to January. She's glad she missed Christmas, imagine spending it alone. Christmas with Asante and Bakari was hard enough — present, yet not present.

Logic would suggest she jumps again, further into the past, but she's literally running out of time. If she doesn't hook up with Green before his first jump, then who knows what will happen. The Tesseract is set for the triggering effect that happened in 1990. And, if the time jump hasn't happened to Green further back, how the hell could he ever believe her? And what would she be fixing, if it hadn't yet happened? She needs his trust to do what she must do. She can't risk getting it wrong.

Anyway, Melbourne's alright. The culture capital even this far into the past. Shops and malls all around the Sarah Sands in New Brunswick. Not the worst place to hang a while to gather her thoughts. She loves shopping, trying out this era's fashion. She buys a pleather jacket, but keeps sneakers from 2018. She's not sure about a tiny slip dress, an evening number, but she takes it anyhow. It's not as flimsy as the sheer maxis Tula tormented her with. She grabs jeans and tees too, and, damn, they look good on her.

The future already tells her she'll attend Sharee and Will's wedding. She wonders about cause and effect. How much of the future might change if she doesn't show up at that wedding…? If she never first meets Sharee at the wedding, how would it affect their encounter in the future?

But Zada has another reason. Her attending the wedding is not for the mission. She wants to see Sharee again, the woman who reminds her of Asante.

The 90s are so backward. She's kept the room above the Sarah Sands, although it's little more than a pub and much more rough and ready. Downstairs the walls are painted black. There's a barman called Sinner who has taken an interest she's not reciprocating.

She's occupied, walks the streets looking for Green. Hangs at the bar during club nights. Increasingly, she's more of a viewer than a participator. Keeps away from the dance floor. Those who drift in and out of her vision are but actors on a stage. She sees them only in the moment. Her heritage doesn't mean she knows their futures. She's a deposit of oil floating on water.

She'd trialled a few mini jumps to get here. She timed one around the date when Green's SocialBox broadcasts started — even then, the timing was stuffed. Once, she could have sworn, she glimpsed him near the Diplomat, but her mind is playing tricks. She no longer trusts memory or history. How funny — well *not* funny: future or history? Perhaps that fever messed with her head. If she saw Green, then she'd lost him again. She's running in circles. Face after face after face. It's like scanning through online dating, never finding a match.

Chapter 29

Zada fixes her make-up. Cosmetics in this age aren't as right for her skin colour. Even cosmopolitan Melbourne has yet to completely embrace—or acknowledge—ethnicity. She hasn't experienced any outright prejudice, but stereotypes abound. Bruces and Sheilas. John would love it here. His anthropology degree put to the test. She wonders what Tula would think. Would she approve of her look?

The face that gazes back at her from the mirror is younger. She puts herself at around 23, maybe? Even A I Green hadn't predicted that she would age backwards. The years shed aren't immediately comparable with those she's travelled through. Something's fucked up.

The house on Turner Street is still that big, grey period structure with flowered awnings, but it's clear they're newlyweds yet to imprint their personalities on the decor. Zada takes a taxi to the reception.

The party has spilled out onto the front lawn. She can smell the barbie from the back through to the front. Zada's unsurprised that Sharee knows a lot of people, but this gathering is quite something considering there can't be anyone from Will's side of the family. Dress is casual and Zada has tried to predict the vibe, so she doesn't look out of place in blue jeans and a knotted tee. Three guys cooing over a motorcycle barely pay her a glance as she walks to the porch. 'That Ain't Bad' by Ratcat plays on the stereo, Zada's heard it enough times at the Sarah Sands to recognise the tune. No-one here knows that Bryan Adams will run more weeks in the chart, but she does. She doesn't know what to do with that information.

Entering the house darkens the scene. The light is so bright outside it throws rooms into shadow. Zada is familiar with the layout. She pauses in the kitchen, takes stock. Dips a Dorito into guacamole and takes a crispy bite. Through the window, into the garden, she can see Sharee now. Out of the wedding dress and in a green playsuit, a blue chiffon shirt flowering around her arms. Zada pauses—a second Dorito to her mouth. There's a bohemian openness to Sharee that makes Zada ache for Asante. If she can't return to the future, could she park herself here, take Sharee and Will as surrogate parents? Perhaps wait for Green to turn up in six months—or whatever—would that be so bad?

Bateman had it right. Nostalgia for the future.

She doesn't at first recognise Will when he enters the kitchen. Then for a brief moment he reminds her of Green. He's tall, a good-looker in a rugged sort of way. Perhaps it's the pierce in his eyes. Or the set of his jaw. He drops the empties he's carrying into the sink. He grins at her. He has a smile on him as big as the Yarra. He knows he's just married the woman he wants.

"Hey," he says.

Zada holds out her hand. Will takes it and they shake. This is the closest she has ever gotten to Green.

"Hey. Zada."

"Will. The...groom...the husband," he laughs, stumbling over his new role. "Been together a while, still it takes some getting used to. You a friend of Sharee's?"

"We've met," Zada says. "Me and Sharee."

She's cryptic, and she knows it. How to explain to Will all that stuff about the future? Instead, she says, "I'm looking for Green."

Will's brow furrows. A cloud crosses the sun. "Yeah, that one. Didn't show up at the wedding. He say he was coming here?"

Zada shakes her head. "Not exactly. But I know that he planned to. If he didn't make it, then he'd have his reasons."

Will nods. There's sorrow in his eyes now, and Zada feels guilty for placing it there. Then he looks hopeful. "Are you... he...?"

Zada allows herself a smile. "Maybe, I'm working on it," she says. "Who knows the cards in the future?"

Will opens the fridge, pulls out a six-pack, unhooks one from the ring and hands it to her. "Should be a stubby holder around here, if you can find one. These cans are ice cold."

Zada nods.

Will carries the other beers out of the kitchen, puts a friendly hand on her shoulder as he passes.

"If you see my boy," he says, "take good care of him."

"You sound sure that I might."

"Find him, take care of him, or both?" He winks at her. "What are you young for? Leave us ol' bastards—go get him."

Then he's back in the sunshine, and Zada sees Sharee studying her through the window. She's wearing a half-smile, an almost knowing look that unsettles Zada. The older woman laughs as Will snakes an arm around her waist, distracts her from Zada.

Zada takes out the Tesseract from her purse.

Chapter 30

Zada is despondent. She's managed to miss Green everywhere. How is this man so impossible to find? It feels deliberate—he's eluding her. What if he's watching somewhere, chuckling at her efforts to find him? She imagines him in cahoots with A I Green. That would be a laugh and a half. Bateman's words ring in her mind over and over, the bloody elephant in her room. "So what happens if you miss Green?"

Well, what happens is that the mission is fucked.

She's tough and she's brave, she consoles herself. Like those rookies at the G. Pulling triggers with a boot, straight through the middle. She's got this. She'll fight to the end.

She goes to the footy. But the MCG isn't the same without Bateman. The players are sharp to come to the field. They are strikers, happy to take the heat. Rookies gobbled up in savage tackles. Rookies coughing up the ball. They snap goals that split the middle, each kick with plenty on it. They get underneath the ball, bang on the boot, or massage it gently to a pretty good finish. She sees how they use their bodies to find the right spots. They're not lost like her.

This one gets to the ball first, ribs out, squeezes one through. *Goal!*

The crowd feeds on it, bopping in the aisles. Commentators crying: "Hits it well, hits it really well!" Another player nurses the ball home, "Oh, you beaut!" It doesn't help that it's a home away game, Brisbane Lions and Sydney Swans. That Brissie's in the mix reminds her too much of Batey. "Got his afternoon boots on!" The striker is technical and brave. He has dancing feet, rolling, rolling after the footy. Kicks the ball as far as he can.

Commentators going:

"It's coming, the ball is coming—it's great!"

"Imagine that!"

In the pulse of a crowd, roaring as the striker nails a goal, and another, she's alone.

She watches morosely as a rookie limps off the pitch. He's all ripped, wearing one eyebrow. What he needs is a patch, running repairs. But, even from the bench, she can see on the big screen how he's wistfully contemplating the pitch. Eager to collect goals, bouncing to break the other team's heart.

She feels heartbreak. Isolation. Disruption. Nothing in her life is going in emphatic straight lines. She wishes she could go turn, snap, *goal!* Reshape her path. The universe going, "Shapes it beautifully!"

Chapter 31

Her sense of loss is harder at night, back at the Sarah Sands, sooty fingers poking into her space and time. But the world refuses to stay black and white—she'd handle it better without all those hues, gazillion shades of uncertainty. This world's unsoft art belongs in a gallery of inky monsters outside a star's tale. A star in a system she's yet to understand. She looks and sees gaps inside an absence that is still, a non-appearance interminably locked in her existence. Unsafely, unreasonably sealed in—she can't escape it.

During the day, Melbourne and the retail therapy it offers don't help. Zada is back to walking the city, scrutinising faces in the streets, at the train station, on the bus. She nearly goes to Essendon, but can't bring herself to bear one more disappointment. Each disenchantment now feels like a nail in her coffin.

Dragging her feet back towards the Sarah Sands Hotel, she sees why Green would describe it as a giant square cake with windows, a cake that stands on the tarmac. She'd gobble it, bite after bite, if it would solve her quest.

What now?

Unlike those rookies at the MCG, nothing can set her right. She has the hunger, but that's about all. What she's dragging are running reports of failure. She's failed everyone who relied on her. Green too, who doesn't even know it—the extent of her flop. She's awkward in this world. She doesn't belong here.

And now she's stuck here.

It's dusk. She showers, makes herself up, slips into the tiny slip dress, anything to perk up her mood. She throws the pleather jacket over it, guides her feet into sneakers from the future. She goes downstairs to where she can smell the steak, it's divine, but she's not hungry. What she's hungry for, the kitchen can't provide.

She even indulges Sinner a little at the bar, chats with him some, but her mind isn't there.

"Champagne cocktail?" he offers. "On the house."

"Maybe later."

Zada looks around. This is it, that's how it feels like. The last stop. She has no way back or forward in time. The Tesseract should close history here, in Green's furthermost place, the homing place where his time jumps began.

The bouncers give her no dramas, act like they really like her. Most men do. Most girls don't. Except Tula.

Zada looks at the hookers scowling at her. They're dressed in hip-hop, baggy jeans and tank tops. Frowning at her when they aren't trying too hard to catch the attention of blokes wearing platform shoes and studded belts.

She *feels* him before she sees him.

It's like an energy pulse that grows stronger, to overwhelming intensity. By the time he reaches the bar and catches Sinner's eye, Zada's nearly exploding from the heat.

Heavens, she's going to faint.

She takes time to compose herself, arrange her face to something near normal. Breathe, she says to herself. Breathe.

How does one hitch up with a guy in this era? she wonders. In the future, you swipe left or right. But he's already looking in her direction. Looking at *her*. She sees on his face what she sees when the bouncers eye her, when Sinner eyes her.

Green smiles *at her*. "You look like an Em. New?"

She smiles back, at his English accent. "Something like that." It's like looking at a younger Will, those piercing eyes, the shape of his jaw...

She feels an inescapable connection, it's like how she felt with Bateman, only this...It's different. *Stronger* is the understatement of the century.

"Try the Sea Breeze," he says. "It's ace."

She pretends to lean over the counter, feigns to ignore him. She beckons Sinner. "How about..." she looks at Green, "not a Sea Breeze?"

"Say what you want," says Sinner, not playing ball. A bit sour about that champagne cocktail.

She points at the fluorescent drink that a girl is balancing on a tray as she walks from the counter. "I'll have one of that."

"It's a Woo Woo," says Green.

"Sure thing. Now you're naming drinks?"

Sinner mixes, shakes, pours, and pushes the flute. Zada turns to Green. "I'm gonna need you to pay for this."

Doesn't chivalry always work?

"I can feel the pressure," Green teases, reaches for his wallet.

"How about I get it?" a man says behind him.

"Yeah, first dibs," says Zada, hoping that Green will battle for chivalry.

Instead, he just smiles. "Close call," he says. "Stay in touch."

He downs his crisp vodka, and turns away from the bar. Above, DJ Shazam is doing his shuffles. Zada watches Green take the dance floor. He throws his hands, pumps his body to the wink of the lights.

She watches how he adjusts his body in jeans and an oversized flannel shirt. How he anticipates the music, the lights, each blink and flash of the strobes. She downs her Woo Woo, shrugs off her jacket. She takes the Tesseract from her clutch purse, puts it in the cleft of her breast, where the bra holds. She wraps the jacket around her sunnies and purse. She pushes the roll-up toward Sinner. "Watch this for me, will ya?"

"Sure thing." He shoves them under the counter.

She finds Green, easy. He's swaying to the beats, nearly not solo, as a hooker is on the hunt, sashaying nearer and nearer towards Green.

"Scoring points?" Zada says across his shoulder.

Green swirls. "You dropped in."

"Deep. You said to stay in touch. I didn't know how so this is the next best thing."

She slips next to him, flows to the music. "You're not trying," she says.

"Trust me, I'm an expert."

"Of what—guessing girls' names? We both know how that went."

She slow dances on the spot in a grind and sway. "Nice," he says. "You mean business."

"You like naming things—what's this move, then?"

"The Rage."

They laugh.

DJ Shazam whizzes out a fast-paced renegade, some megamix, the chords of 'Kool Thing' chime. Green does a butterfly move, and Zada quiver dances to the throb of his pulse. It's just them, the rest of the dance floor out of it in that moment.

Zada puts her hand on her breast. She feels the Tesseract. It's now or never.

"Look," Green leans across the music just as she touches the reset button on the Tesseract. A bright flash throws her like a blast, then she's out.

Chapter 32

She comes to on a bed, Sinner's bunk behind the bar. "You good?" He looks concerned.

"What happened?"

"I don't know. You were dancing, then collapsed. Here's your things. No pressure."

She sits up in alarm—instinct. She mentally checks herself over. Yeah, Sinner's one of the good guys. Someone else might have taken advantage. She manages a smile and he lets her be, returns to the bar while she composes herself. She can hear the music thudding through the wall.

Later, she's sat at a table near the pool table, chatting to some girls she's just met. They're yapping foolishly, as young girls do, asking her questions about her sneakers and outfit, as if they're life and death. One of the girls, a sweet-looking one, smells like a wet goat. A man with spiked black-as-black hair walks past looking in her direction, then away. He enters the men's toilet.

Green! Recollection slowly returns. She feels for the Tesseract. She's not sure it worked. Is Green reset? She looks at the Tesseract. Bloody hell. It's causal.

She's the damn root cause.

She and her Tesseract triggered Green's time jumps in the first place. A causal loop! And only she can fix it.

"See yas!" she pushes back her chair, stands from the table.

"Whatever," goat girl says.

Zada stands outside the toilet. She wonders if she should go in. Now she panics. He's taking a long time coming out. Damn! She found and lost Green. The door opens. It's not Green, just some punk. The door opens. Green. He stops short, as if thinking about it. Then a tentative smile as he approaches her.

"It's me," she says.

"Of course, it's you. I thought you forgot."

"I mean *it's me*. My fault. What happened on the dance floor."

"Woah. Time out."

"Exactly. I'm the reason you're time jumping."

"What?"

"The Tesseract cube, I reset it to the wrong dimension. I needed to work on your third dimension."

"I have no clue whatsoever," he says. "But I'll listen better if you dance with me."

"Okay. I guess we need to start from the *start*."

"Why not?"

"And we need to go over the sequence."

"Why?" he says. And kisses her.

His lips are white chocolate and apricot. Her head feels weightless, their heartbeats together. He feels like home, which is confusing. Because Green…Green is here. And home…home is Tula. Yet Zada has never felt like this before, at home, secure. She's never wanted this badly to stay, not to run. To be with someone, like this, forever. To grow old together.

But he pulls back almost immediately, the kiss not enough. She wants more.

"We'd better ask the DJ for a special request," he murmurs against her lips.

"Yes," she says. "Why don't you ask him?"

He brushes her lips and his fingers stroke across her waist as he leaves.

She takes the Tesseract. It didn't work on the 7th dimension. He'll time jump any minute and she'll lose him forever. She turns the cubes to the right dial, and the music is already playing. 'Kool Thing'.

Now it's just the two of them on the dance floor. They are not the beats of a slow dance, but they are slow dancing. Rubbing and swaying, more like. Kissing.

His eyes make love to her on the dance floor. She's ready to give him everything.

"I don't know much about you," he murmurs.

"Green," she whispers back. "My name is Zada. I come from the future. And I'm sorry."

She resets the Tesseract.

Chapter 33

I come to in a backyard. I look down at my small hands and the smocking dress I'm wearing. It's handmade. I can't remember where or why I'm here in the back of a house littered with black bamboo, a veggie patch and a loquat tree.

I turn towards the noise coming from inside the house. Then I remember. My new adoptive parents: Graham and Jean. Their racket is not from a fight. It's the sound that follows their yoga. It tugs a memory I can't quite access.

But there's a new noise, and it's not coming from my house. It's across the fence next door. I put a hand on the fence, push myself up. I look out at the small boy in shorts. He has black-as-black hair. He meets my stare with a piercing gaze that's not unpleasant.

I grin at him. "I'm Zada. You look like you got a name."

He says nothing, just piercing eyes taking me in.

"You got a name on you, or what?" I press.

He seems to think about it for a moment, weighing whether he's got a name, or if he should give it.

When he speaks, it's not an answer to my question. Instead, he says, "That's a bit of a din." He nods towards my house.

"Least not yowling like from yours. Shall we help them kill each other?"

He contemplates me, smiles a little.

"Nah. They do a better job themselves." He pauses. As though deciding whether to offer up a secret. "Green. That's my name."

I smile wider. I remember.

I know.

Author Biographies

Eugen Bacon is an African Australian author of several novels and fiction collections. She's a finalist in the 2022 World Fantasy Award. Her recent books *Ivory's Story*, *Danged Black Thing* and *Saving Shadows* are finalists in the British Science Fiction Association (BSFA) Awards. Eugen was announced in the honour list of the 2022 Otherwise Fellowships for "doing exciting work in gender and speculative fiction". She has won, been longlisted or commended in international awards, including the Aurealis Award, Foreword Indies, Bridport Prize, Copyright Agency Prize, Horror Writers Association Diversity Grant, Otherwise, Rhysling, Australian Shadows, Ditmar Awards and Nommo Awards for Speculative Fiction by Africans. Eugen's creative work has appeared in literary and speculative fiction publications worldwide, including *Award Winning Australian Writing*, *Fantasy Magazine*, *Fantasy & Science Fiction* and *Year's Best African Speculative Fiction*. New books in 2022: *Mage of Fools* (Meerkat Press), *Chasing Whispers* (Raw Dog Screaming Press) and *An Earnest Blackness* (Anti-Oedipus Press). Visit her website at eugenbacon.com and Twitter @EugenBacon

Andrew Hook is a European writer who has been published extensively in the independent press since 1994 in a variety of genres, with over 160 short stories in print, including notable appearances in *Interzone*, *Black Static*, and several anthologies from PS Publishing and NewCon Press. His fiction has been reprinted in anthologies including *Best British Horror 2015* and *Best British Short Stories 2020*, has been shortlisted for British Fantasy Society awards, and he was longlisted for the Commonwealth Writers Short Story Prize in 2020. As editor/ publisher, he has won three British Fantasy Society awards and he also has been a judge for the World Fantasy Awards. Most recent publications include several noir crime novels through Head Shot Press, a novella written in collaboration with the legendary San Francisco art collective known as The Residents, and his tenth short story collection, *Candescent Blooms* (Salt Publishing). He can be found at www.andrew-hook.com or Twitter @AndrewHookUK

FANTASY, SCI-FI, HORROR & PARANORMAL

If you prefer to spend your nights with Vampires and Werewolves rather than the mundane then we publish the books for you. If your preference is for Dragons and Faeries or Angels and Demons – we should be your first stop. Perhaps your perfect partner has artificial skin or comes from another planet – step right this way. If your passion is Fantasy (including magical realism and spiritual fantasy), Metaphysical Cosmology, Horror or Science Fiction (including Steampunk), Cosmic Egg books will feed your hunger. Our curiosity shop contains treasures you will enjoy unearthing. If you have enjoyed this book, why not tell other readers by posting a review on your preferred book site.

Recent bestsellers from Cosmic Egg Books are:

The Zombie Rule Book
A Zombie Apocalypse Survival Guide
Tony Newton
The book the living-dead don't want you to have!
Paperback: 978-1-78279-334-2 ebook: 978-1-78279-333-5

Cryptogram
Because the Past is Never Past
Michael Tobert
Welcome to the dystopian world of 2050, where three lovers
are haunted by echoes from eight-hundred years ago.
Paperback: 978-1-78279-681-7 ebook: 978-1-78279-680-0

Purefinder
Ben Gwalchmai
London, 1858. A child is dead; a man is blamed and dragged
through hell in this Dantean tale of loss, mystery and
fraternity.
Paperback: 978-1-78279-098-3 ebook: 978-1-78279-097-6

600ppm
A Novel of Climate Change
Clarke W. Owens
Nature is collapsing. The government doesn't want you to
know why. Welcome to 2051 and 600ppm.
Paperback: 978-1-78279-992-4 ebook: 978-1-78279-993-1

Creations
William Mitchell
Earth 2040 is on the brink of disaster. Can Max Lowrie stop the
self-replicating machines before it's too late?
Paperback: 978-1-78279-186-7 ebook: 978-1-78279-161-4

The Gawain Legacy
Jon Mackley
If you try to control every secret, secrets may end up
controlling you.
Paperback: 978-1-78279-485-1 ebook: 978-1-78279-484-4

Readers of ebooks can buy or view any of these bestsellers by
clicking on the live link in the title. Most titles are published
in paperback and as an ebook. Paperbacks are available in
traditional bookshops. Both print and ebook formats are
available online.
Find more titles and sign up to our readers' newsletter at
http://www.johnhuntpublishing.com/fiction
Follow us on Facebook at https://www.facebook.com/JHPFiction
and Twitter at https://twitter.com/JHPFiction